WALT DISNEY'S

UNCLE SCROOGE

The Grand Canyon Conquest

The Grand Canyon Conquest

Writer & Artist: Miquel Pujol
Inkers: Celeste Parramón & Maite López Espí
Colorist: Ehapa Verlag GmbH & Digikore Studios
Letterers: Tom B. Long and Travis and Nicole Seitler
Translation & Dialogue: Gary Leach

Heights of Fear

Writer: Evert Geradts
Artist: Bas Heymans
Colorist: Digikore Studios
Letterers: Travis and Nicole Seitler
Translation & Dialogue: Maura McManus

Belle Corners the Coin Collection

Artist: Al Hubbard
Colorist: Disney Italia with Digikore Studios
Letterer: Tom B. Long

Going Places

Writer: Alberto Savini
Artist: Andrea Freccero
Colorist: Disney Italia with David Gerstein
Letterer: Travis Seitler
Translation & Dialogue: David Gerstein

Special thanks to Curt Baker, Julie Dorris, Manny Mederos, Beatrice Osman, Roberto Santillo, Camilla Vedove, Stefano Ambrosio, and Carlotta Quattrocolo.

ISBN: 978-1-63140-475-7

18 17 16 15   1 2 3 4

IDW®
www.IDWPUBLISHING.com
IDW founded by Ted Adams, Alex Garner, Kris Oprisko, and Robbie Robbins

Ted Adams, CEO & Publisher
Greg Goldstein, President & COO
Robbie Robbins, EVP/Sr. Graphic Artist
Chris Ryall, Chief Creative Officer/Editor-in-Chief
Matthew Ruzicka, CPA, Chief Financial Officer
Alan Payne, VP of Sales
Dirk Wood, VP of Marketing
Lorelei Bunjes, VP of Digital Services
Jeff Webber, VP of Digital Publishing & Business Development

Facebook: facebook.com/idwpublishing
Twitter: @idwpublishing
YouTube: youtube.com/idwpublishing
Tumblr: tumblr.idwpublishing.com
Instagram: instagram.com/idwpublishing

Originally published as UNCLE SCROOGE issues #4-6 (Legacy #408-410).

Series Editor: Sarah Gaydos
Archival Editor: David Gerstein

Cover Artist: Miquel Pujol
Cover Colorist: David Gerstein
Collection Editors: Justin Eisinger
                    & Alonzo Simon
Collection Designer: Clyde Grapa

Art by Miquel Pujol, Colors by Scott Rockwell

TODAY'S WEATHER REPORT PREDICTED A STORMY NIGHT FOR DUCKBURG! LOOKS LIKE THAT FORECAST WAS ON THE NOSE!

BAWOOM

WALT DISNEY'S

UNCLE SCROOGE

THE GRAND CANYON CONQUEST!

DONALD DUCK

SOME DENIZENS BARELY NOTICE...

...WHILE OTHERS, WELL...

I HEREBY SENTENCE YOU TO *LIFE* AT *UNPAID HARD LABOR* FOR SCROOGE McDUCK!

MERCY, JUDGE! DON'T SEND ME BACK TO THAT TYRANT—

YOU *HEARD* MY RULING! NOW *SKEDADDLE!*

WHAM... WHAM...

⇒PHEW!⇐ WHAT A NIGHTMARE! THAT COURTROOM, THAT POUNDING GAVEL...

WHAM...

WHAM...

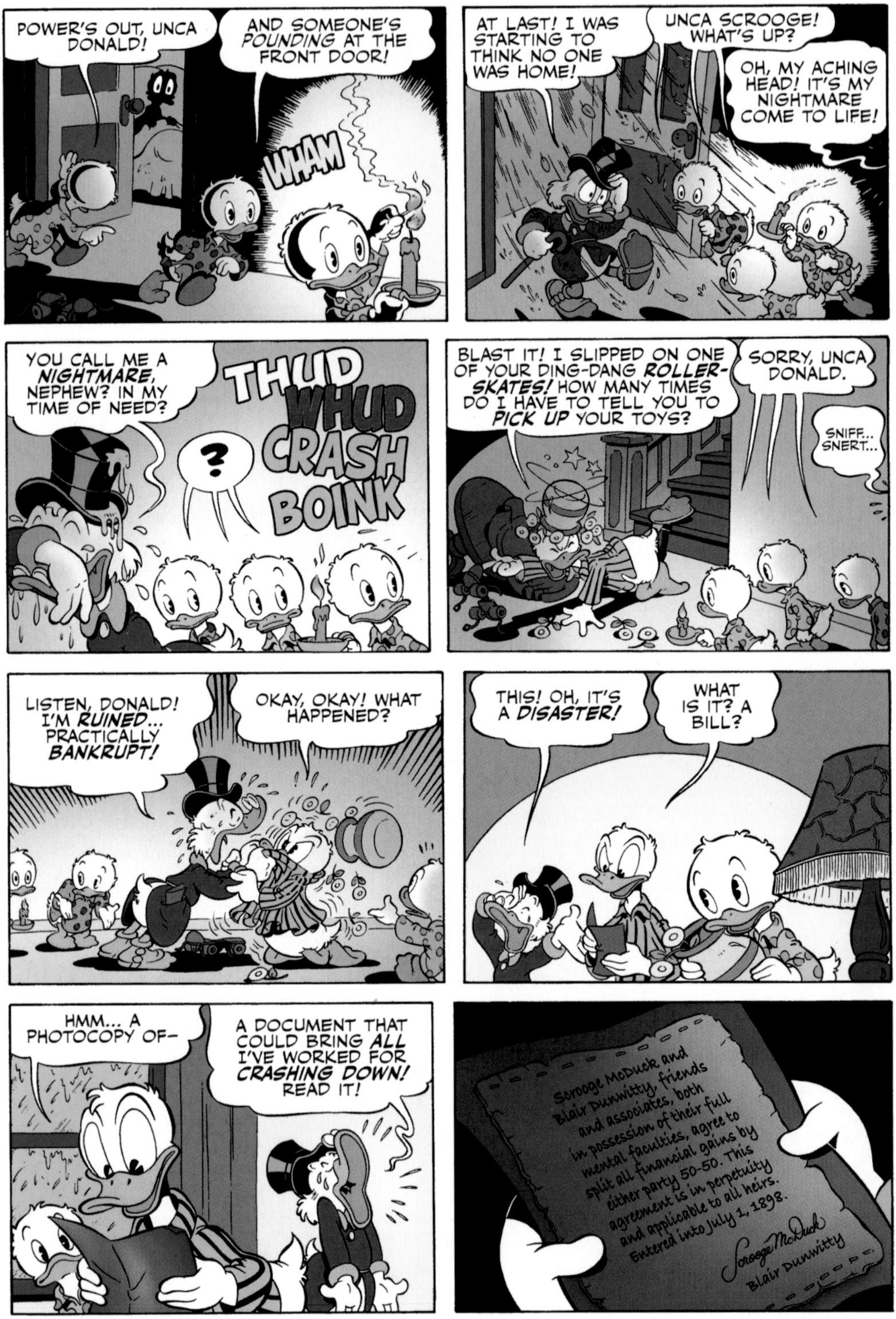
POWER'S OUT, UNCA DONALD!
AND SOMEONE'S *POUNDING* AT THE FRONT DOOR!
WHAM
AT LAST! I WAS STARTING TO THINK NO ONE WAS HOME!
UNCA SCROOGE! WHAT'S UP?
OH, MY ACHING HEAD! IT'S MY NIGHTMARE COME TO LIFE!
YOU CALL ME A ***NIGHTMARE***, NEPHEW? IN MY TIME OF NEED?
THUD
WHUD
CRASH
BOINK
?
BLAST IT! I SLIPPED ON ONE OF YOUR DING-DANG ***ROLLER-SKATES!*** HOW MANY TIMES DO I HAVE TO TELL YOU TO ***PICK UP*** YOUR TOYS?
SORRY, UNCA DONALD.
SNIFF... SNERT...
LISTEN, DONALD! I'M ***RUINED***... PRACTICALLY ***BANKRUPT!***
OKAY, OKAY! WHAT HAPPENED?
THIS! OH, IT'S A ***DISASTER!***
WHAT IS IT? A BILL?
HMM... A PHOTOCOPY OF–
A DOCUMENT THAT COULD BRING ***ALL*** I'VE WORKED FOR ***CRASHING DOWN!*** READ IT!
Scrooge McDuck and Blair Dunwitty, friends and associates, both in possession of their full mental faculties, agree to split all financial gains by either party 50-50. This agreement is in perpetuity and applicable to all heirs. Entered into July 1, 1898.
Scrooge McDuck
Blair Dunwitty

BUT 1898 WAS *AGES* AGO, UNCA SCROOGE! AND *WE'RE* YOUR HEIRS! *WE'D* NEVER TRY TO RUIN YOU!

YEAH, SO WHAT'S THE PROBLEM?

YOU DON'T UNDERSTAND! *ANOTHER* HEIR HAS TURNED UP! HE SAYS HE'S *OWEN* DUNWITTY, *NEPHEW* OF MY OLD ASSOCIATE!

CAREFUL OF THAT *SKATE.*

FOR A FACT?

HE CAME TO ME WITH THE ORIGINAL OF THE AGREEMENT! HE KNOWS TOO MUCH ABOUT MY CORPORATE STRUCTURE... AND *DEMANDS 50%* OF ALL MY *HOLDINGS!* I'M *DESTITUTE!*

WELL— *HALF* DESTITUTE, ANYWAY!

IT'S NO JOKE! BUT IF YOU DON'T WANT TO HELP, CONSIDER ME GONE!

HELP AT *THIS* HOUR? WHEN THE COWS HAVE COME HOME *AND* BEEN MILKED BY NOW? MOO!

YOU REJECT *ME*, YOUR *DEAR* UNCLE? WHO HAS NEVER FAILED TO PROVIDE AID IN TIMES OF NEED? ⸮SNIFF! SNEEF!⸮ HOW UNGRATEFUL!

YOUR AID ALWAYS COMES WITH A VERY *HIGH* PRICE TAG!

BUT UNCA DONALD, THIS IS ALL ABOUT FAMILY...

...AND IT *SOUNDS* LIKE UNCA SCROOGE...

THANKS, BOYS.

...REALLY *NEEDS* US!

FEH!

⸮ARRR!⸮ WHY DO I ALWAYS WIND UP BEING THE BAD GUY?

WATCH OUT! THE ROLL—

⸮WHOOLP!⸮

WHOOSH

JUST IN TIME!

I HAD NO IDEA YOU'D BE IN SUCH A *HURRY* TO GET GOING!

SO WHO **WAS** BLAIR DUNWITTY, UNCA SCROOGE?

WELL, BOYS, HE WAS A GOOD JOE...

...A STALWART COMRADE, AND GENEROUS TO A FAULT! WE WERE SO ALIKE...

WHAT HO, BLAIR! WE'RE **HERE!**

THAT'S GREAT, SCROOGE!

SO ALIKE, RIGHT...

"BY THE TURN OF THE CENTURY WE'D BEEN THROUGH A LOT TOGETHER, SHARING ROUGH TIMES AND EVEN OUR LAST BREAD. IT WAS THEN..."

SURE NICE TO GET THIS SECOND-HAND JACKET SO CHEAP!

I ALWAYS GIVE MY **FRIENDS** A **DISCOUNT!**

"...WE WROTE UP THAT AGREEMENT ON AN OLD PIECE OF LEATHER, NOT KNOWING IF WE'D **EVER** HAVE ANYTHING WORTH DIVIDING..."

WE WERE ONE FOR ALL THEN, BLAIR AND I!

BEFORE IT WAS ALL FOR **YOU!**

"EVENTUALLY, OUR GOALS IN LIFE HAVING DIVERGED, WE WENT OUR SEPARATE WAYS! WE WANTED TO **MAINTAIN** OUR AGREEMENT—BUT, LACKING ENOUGH LEATHER TO UPDATE IT, WE DID IT **ORALLY**... AS WAS COMMON AMONG THE NATIVES!"

DO YOU AGREE TO THE REVISED SPLIT, BLAIR?

AMEN, BROTHER!

BEFORE WE PARTED, BLAIR ASKED TO **KEEP** THE FIRST DRAFT OF OUR AGREEMENT AS A **MEMENTO** OF OUR FRIENDSHIP! I AGREED—

IN EXCHANGE FOR YOUR GOLD MINES!

THAT'S A BIT STEEP, BUT I CONSIDER OUR FRIENDSHIP PRICELESS!

AS **ALIKE** AS YOU WERE, UNK, I'M SURE YOU LEFT HIM ONE CANTEEN OF WATER AND A PIECE OF BREAD SO HE WOULDN'T STARVE!

WHY WOULD I DO THAT, NEPHEW? I'D ALREADY GIVEN HIM MY MATCHES!

SOON, IN SCROOGE'S OFFICE!

OWEN DUNWITTY'S STILL WAITING FOR YOU, MR. McDUCK. I COULDN'T GET HIM TO LEAVE. BUT CAN *I* GO HOME NOW?

SIT TIGHT, MISS QUACKFASTER! I'LL JUST BE A MINUTE!

DONE WITH YOUR MIDNIGHT RAMBLE, PARTNER?

PARTNER?! GET *OUT* OF MY CHAIR!

CHAIR? AH, THIS VINYL OFFICE LOUNGER YOU BOUGHT IN 1972! HALF-MINE!

¿GRROWR!¿

COOL IT, UNCLE SCROOGE!

COOL IT? WHEN THIS CON MAN KNOWS *EVERY* MOVE I EVER MADE?!

YOU SHOULDN'T GET SO WORKED UP AT YOUR AGE. AND FACTS *ARE* FACTS!

I'LL GET AS WORKED UP AS I *LIKE*, YOU SORRY WASTE OF SPACE!

OKAY! BUT DON'T SAY I DIDN'T WARN YOU!

WHAT DO YOU THINK?

HARD TO *SAY* AT THIS POINT...

I'M GLAD YOU'RE HERE, MR. McDUCK! SOMETHING DREADFUL HAS HAPPENED!

WHAT IS IT NOW?

I GUESS WE'RE DONE FOR THE MOMENT, SO I'LL BE BACK IN THE MORNING! CAN'T WAIT TO SEE HOW *OUR* BUSINESSES ARE DOING!

I'M AFRAID THIS IS *ABOUT* ONE OF YOUR BUSINESSES, SIR!

GREAT GOBBLING GANDERS!

HOTEL GROUP
Income: $104,563,842
Outgo: $111,563,842
Deficit: $7,000,000

THIS IS CATASTROPHIC! HOW DID IT HAPPEN?

NOT SURE, SIR! YOUR HOTELS GENERALLY DO WELL! THOUGH THERE IS THAT ONE IN BEVERLY HILLS...

...THAT *HASN'T* BEEN PERFORMING UP TO EXPECTATIONS!

DOWN AND OUT IN BEVERLY HILLS! ⇒GLEEP! PLEEP!⇐

TWO BLOWS IN ONE DAY! IT'S TOO MUCH!

QUICK, MISS QUACKFASTER! *WATER!*

WHAT A NIGHT! I MAY NEVER GET HOME!

AND PEOPLE THINK BUSINESS TYCOONS LEAD SUCH CAREFREE LIVES! ⇒SOB!⇐

CHEER UP, PARTNER! STARTING TOMORROW, YOU'LL HAVE ONLY *HALF* YOUR BUSINESSES TO WORRY ABOUT!

OH, NO...

McD   DUNWITTY

McD   DUNWITTY

I *CAN'T* DO IT! I CAN'T *SHARE* WITH THAT SCALAWAG!

IT'S TOO BAD *BLAIR* DUNWITTY'S GONE! HE'D BE GLAD TO ANNUL THE AGREEMENT RATHER THAN LET THIS HAPPEN TO ME!

ARE WE *SURE* HE'S GONE? MAYBE OWEN *STOLE* THAT DOCUMENT!

YOU'RE RIGHT! THESE ARE QUESTIONS THAT NEED ANSWERS!

YOU EXPECT TO GET 'EM AT *TWO O'CLOCK* IN THE *MORNING?!*

⇒SIGH!⇐ THAT'S *OFTEN* WHEN HE GETS ROLLING!

NO TIME LIKE THE PRESENT! FIRST THING TO DO IS DIG UP BLAIR'S LAST KNOWN ADDRESS!

EXACTLY!

OUR UNCA SCROOGE IS BACK!

BLAIR LEFT THE KLONDIKE TO LIVE WITH HIS *BROTHER* IN LOS ANGELES... ON HOLLYWOOD BOULEVARD! WE'LL START THERE!

WHADDAYA MEAN "WE"? YOU'RE THE NIGHT OWL!

BY "WE" I MEAN *WE!* ON THE NEXT PLANE TO L.A.! IT'LL BE A BUSINESS JUNKET!

A JUNKET WHERE I GET THE *BUSINESS*, I BET!

IF YOU'RE GOING THERE, YOU COULD ALSO CHECK ON THAT BEVERLY HILLS HOTEL!

YOU AND THE BOYS CAN DO THAT, DONALD!

I'LL EVEN COVER THE *COST* OF YOUR STAY. THE *MCDUCK OASIS*... IT'S A POSH PLACE, WITH ALL THE AMENITIES AND FIVE-STAR CUISINE! UNDER *NEW MANAGEMENT* THESE DAYS, SO THEY'LL WANT TO *CURRY FAVOR!* HOW DOES THAT SOUND?

LIKE A *DEAL*, UNK!

I'LL LOCATE BLAIR'S OLD HOLLYWOOD ADDRESS AND TRY TO PICK UP HIS TRAIL!

WELL, IF YOU DON'T NEED *ME* ANYMORE, SIR...

YOU'LL BOOK US ON THE NEXT FLIGHT TO L.A., MISS QUACKFASTER!

WILL I... UH... GET *OVERTIME* FOR THAT?

90

HA! OVERTIME, JUST FOR BEING IN THE OFFICE EXTRA *EARLY?* ABSURD! NOW HOP TO IT!

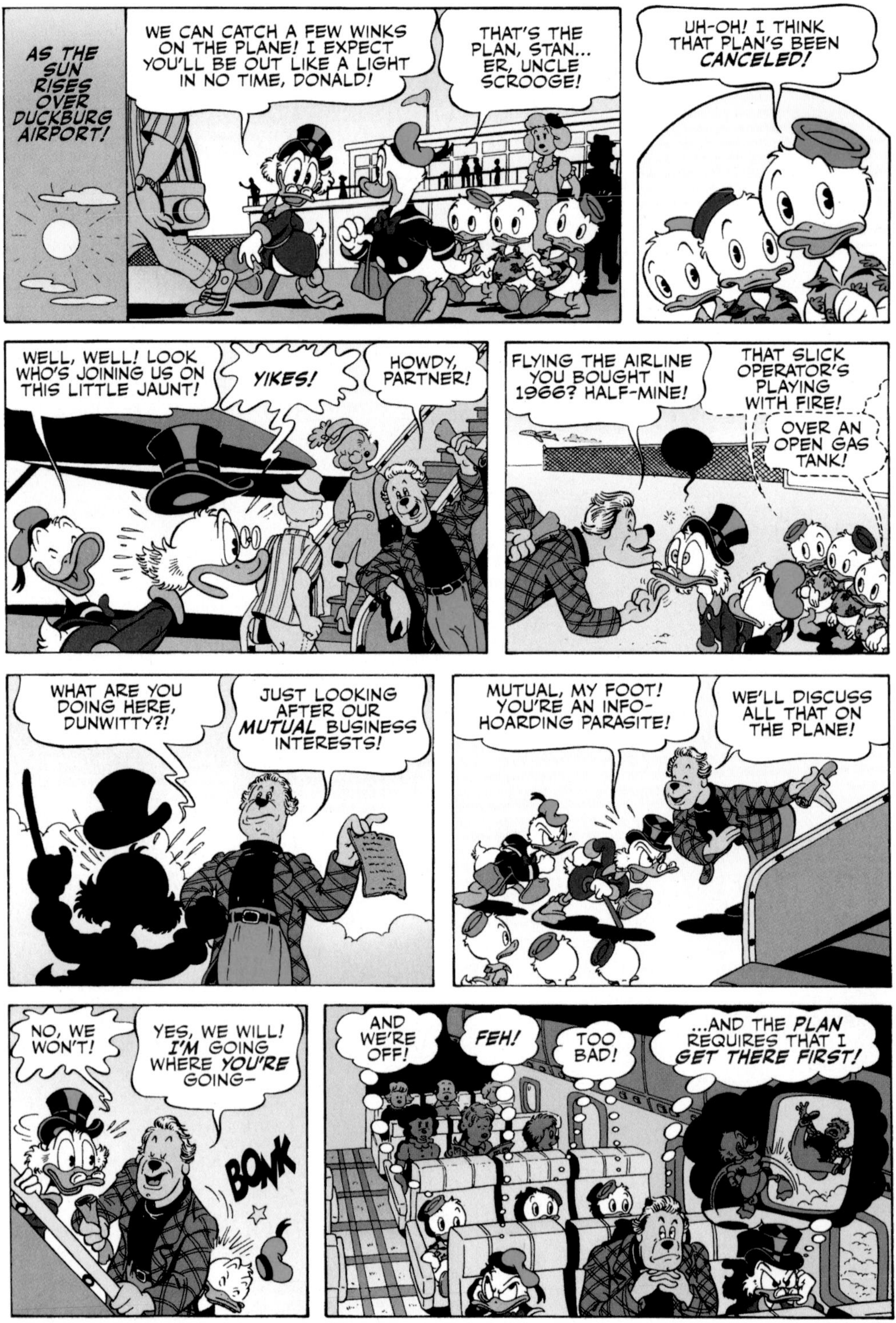
AS THE SUN RISES OVER DUCKBURG AIRPORT!
WE CAN CATCH A FEW WINKS ON THE PLANE! I EXPECT YOU'LL BE OUT LIKE A LIGHT IN NO TIME, DONALD!
THAT'S THE PLAN, STAN... ER, UNCLE SCROOGE!
UH-OH! I THINK THAT PLAN'S BEEN CANCELED!
WELL, WELL! LOOK WHO'S JOINING US ON THIS LITTLE JAUNT!
YIKES!
HOWDY, PARTNER!
FLYING THE AIRLINE YOU BOUGHT IN 1966? HALF-MINE!
THAT SLICK OPERATOR'S PLAYING WITH FIRE!
OVER AN OPEN GAS TANK!
WHAT ARE YOU DOING HERE, DUNWITTY?!
JUST LOOKING AFTER OUR MUTUAL BUSINESS INTERESTS!
MUTUAL, MY FOOT! YOU'RE AN INFO-HOARDING PARASITE!
WE'LL DISCUSS ALL THAT ON THE PLANE!
NO, WE WON'T!
YES, WE WILL! I'M GOING WHERE YOU'RE GOING-
BONK
AND WE'RE OFF!
FEH!
TOO BAD!
...AND THE PLAN REQUIRES THAT I GET THERE FIRST!

"PLAN"? HMM! SOON, IN LOS ANGELES...

WE'LL BE LANDING SHORTLY, LADIES AND GENTLEMEN. PLEASE FASTEN YOUR SEAT BELTS!

AAAAAAH!!

IF YOU'LL EXCUSE ME, I NEED TO GET MY NEPHEWS SITUATED!

SURE! I'LL JUST WAIT HERE!

DONALD, YOU AND THE BOYS GO STRAIGHT TO THE McDUCK OASIS. I'LL CONTACT YOU ONCE I DITCH DUNWITTY!

OKAY! I'LL NEED TAXI FARE!

NOTHING DOING! THE HOTEL ROOM IS FREE, THE REST IS ON YOU! THAT WAS THE DEAL!

I SHOULDA KNOWN!

SO MUCH FOR THAT. AND NOW, DUNWITTY, LET'S— HEY, WHERE'S HE GONE?

GOT BORED WAITING, EH? SUITS ME!

NOW'S MY CHANCE! HEY! TAXI!

ABOUT TIME, OLD SOCK! SO WHERE TO?

?

THAT STINGY, PENNY-PINCHING, TIGHTFISTED OLD—

FORGET IT, UNCA DONALD.

UNCA SCROOGE HAS A LOT...

...ON HIS MIND!

HERE WE ARE!

GOTTA ADMIT, IT *LOOKS* LIKE A PRETTY SWANKY PLACE!

McDUCK OASIS HOTEL

WE HAVE ROOMS RESERVED IN THE NAME OF DUCK!

SORRY, WE'RE FULL UP!

WHAT? MY UNCLE, SCROOGE McDUCK, MADE THE RESERVATION—

YOUR UNCLE'S *MR. McDUCK?* MY *APOLOGIES*, SIR... I'LL GET YOU CHECKED IN IMMEDIATELY!

I *DO* HOPE OUR HOTEL WILL BE TO YOUR LIKING!

I'M SURE IT'LL BE FINE!

BEING RELATIVES OF THE OWNER *DOES* HAVE ITS ADVANTAGES!

THAT GUY WAS PRETTY NERVOUS!

YEAH! AND *SHIFTY!*

BETTER KEEP OUR EYES OPEN!

YOUR BUNGALOW, GENTLEMEN!

WOW! HOW 'BOUT THAT, KIDS?

YES, IT'S VERY NICE!

NOW *THIS* IS THE LIFE! GOTTA GIVE UNCLE SCROOGE CREDIT FOR SETTING US UP HERE!

⊰PSST! PSST!⊱ UNCA DONALD!

?

YOU FORGOT TO *TIP* HIM!

HE'S WAITING!

OH YES, OF COURSE!

THANK YOU, YOUNG MAN! LIVE IT UP!

HUH? A QUARTER?

YOU SAYING THAT AIN'T *ENOUGH?* WHAT DID YOU *EXPECT?*

AT LEAST $10, SIR!

$10! MY POOR, RAPIDLY-EMPTYING WALLET!

THANK *YOU*, SIR!

HOLD ON A SEC, MISTER!

WHO WAS THAT MAN WHO CHECKED US IN?

MR. SKAM, THE NEW MANAGER! HE OFTEN WORKS THE FRONT DESK...

...BUT HE'S USUALLY IN BACK, STUDYING McDUCK *BUSINESS RECORDS!* I THINK HE'S PLANNING SOME *RESTRUCTURING*... SEEING AS WE'VE LOST MONEY FAST SINCE HE CAME ABOARD!

‹HM!‹ THANKS FOR THE INFO!

NOT AT ALL! THAT'LL BE *$20!*

AT DINNERTIME...

WE'RE DINING IN *STYLE* TONIGHT! KING CRAB, T-BONE STEAKS... YOU NAME IT!

YOU REALIZE UNCA SCROOGE *WON'T* BE PAYING, RIGHT?

WE DON'T KNOW WHAT THIS MIGHT COST!

IF I'D ASKED, I'D BE OUT ANOTHER FIVE BUCKS!

DIG ALL THE OLD-TIME *ACTOR IMPERSONATORS!* GROUCHO SNARX, CLARK GOBBLE...

ALL HERE TO POSE WITH TOURISTS! BUSINESS IS BOOMING!

HEY! ISN'T THAT SKAM AT THE BAR?

INTERESTING! ALL THESE WEALTHY GUESTS, YET THE HOTEL RECORDS LOSSES!

EVERYTHING LOOKS AND SMELLS ABSOLUTELY DIVINE! I'M DROOLING!

THEN YOU'LL REALLY SALIVATE OVER THESE DIVINE *MENU PRICES!*

⊰GLEEEP!⊱

HAVE YOU DECIDED, GENTLEMEN?

EH? I'D HAVE SWORN THIS TABLE WAS SEATED!

⊰GROAN!⊱ $45 FOR A LOBSTER TAIL! $12 FOR TOAST! $25 FOR A CHOPPED STEAK, AND *$16* FOR A CARAFE OF *WATER!* THERE OUGHTTA BE A *LAW!*

I SAY WE'VE HIT DESPERATE TIMES, MEN!

YEAH! MY STOMACH'S GROWLING!

GRROWL

WE HAVE NO CHOICE BUT TO DIP INTO OUR TRAVEL RATIONS!

BUT WE FORGOT A CAN OPENER!

MAYBE THERE'S ONE IN THE LOUNGE!

WHILE RETURNING WITH THE NEEDED DEVICE...

NICE OF THE SERVER TO LEND US ONE!

HURRY! I'M—

⇒SHHH!⇐ LISTEN!

GROWL

LOOK AT THAT!

MR. SKAM AND...

..THE SERVER!

RELAX, KOCKIE! I DON'T THINK THOSE DUCKS KNOW ANYTHING! WE JUST NEED TO BE CAREFUL FROM NOW ON!

I'LL SEND 'EM COMPLIMENTARY LEMONADES LACED WITH KNOCKOUT DROPS IF NEED BE!

SKAM IS SHIFTY, JUST LIKE WE THOUGHT! TEN-TO-ONE HE'S BEHIND THE HOTEL'S LOSSES!

AND MAYBE SOMETHING... MORE.

TOAST AND SARDINES! WHAT A LETDOWN!

SORRY! THAT'S ALL WE BROUGHT!

AT LEAST WE DIDN'T FORGET OUR CAMP STOVE!

SO WHATCHA THINK? ARE WE RIGHT ABOUT SKAM, UNCA DONALD?

ON THE LOSSES? YOU BET! AND IT'S ODD HOW HE AND THAT OWEN CLUCK CAME OUT OF THE WOODWORK AT... ONCE.

⇒HMPH!⇐ TORCHWOOD ISN'T ON!

CLICK

BOOM!

SO...WHAT TO DO?

RIGHT NOW I JUST WANT A DECENT DINNER!

UNCA SCROOGE HASN'T CALLED IN! I HOPE NOTHING'S *HAPPENED* TO HIM!

I CAN'T TAKE IT ANYMORE! I'M GOING TO BED! AT LEAST I CAN *DREAM* ABOUT ROAST CHICKEN AND KING CRAB AND ALL THAT!

...AND NOW, THE *MENU* FOR THE WEEKEND...

...ARDENNES HAM ON A BED OF PARISIAN ENDIVE...

THE MORE I WORRY, THE MORE I *EAT!*

LIKE WHEN YOU BOUGHT THAT RESTAURANT CHAIN IN 1973? HALF-MINE!

JUST ACCEPT THAT YOU AND I NOW SHARE A FORTUNE!

NOT *MY* FORTUNE, WE DON'T! JUST YOU WAIT!

I AIM TO FIND BLAIR DUNWITTY AND PUT THIS SORRY MESS TO REST!

STUB-BORN DUCK!

HEY! WHO'S *PAYIN'* FOR THESE BURGERS?

MY *PARTNER* WILL BE HAPPY TO COMPENSATE YOU, MY GOOD MAN!

...OKAY, *SURE*...

AS THE SUN RISES OVER THE CITY OF ANGELS!

I'LL SCOPE OUT THE MANAGER, YOU KEEP AN EYE ON THE SERVER!

YOU GOT IT, CHIEF!

NO SUSPICIOUS DOINGS SO FAR! WONDER IF HE'LL—

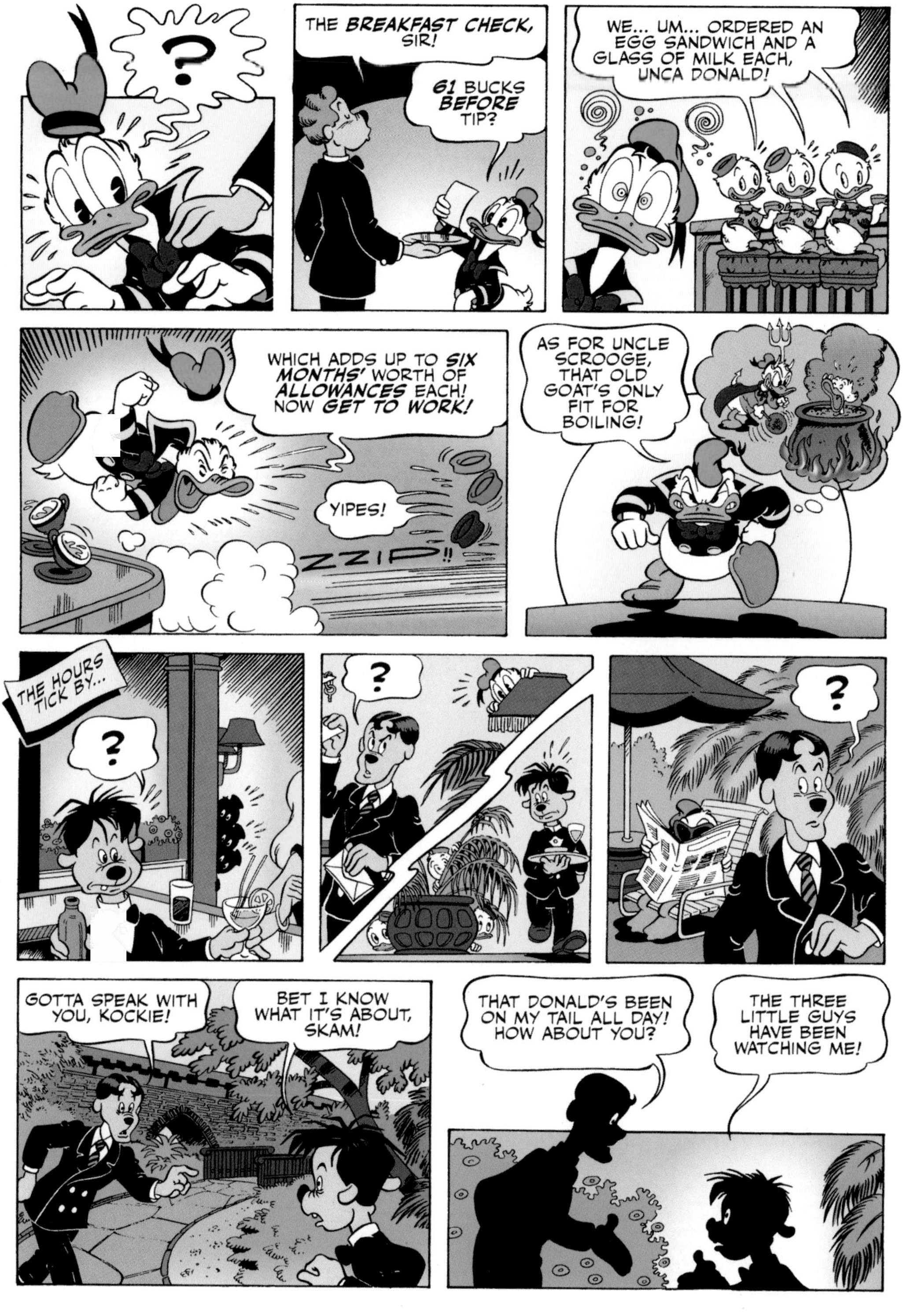
?
THE BREAKFAST CHECK, SIR!
61 BUCKS BEFORE TIP?
WE... UM... ORDERED AN EGG SANDWICH AND A GLASS OF MILK EACH, UNCA DONALD!
WHICH ADDS UP TO SIX MONTHS' WORTH OF ALLOWANCES EACH! NOW GET TO WORK!
YIPES!
ZZIP!!
AS FOR UNCLE SCROOGE, THAT OLD GOAT'S ONLY FIT FOR BOILING!
THE HOURS TICK BY...
?
?
?
GOTTA SPEAK WITH YOU, KOCKIE!
BET I KNOW WHAT IT'S ABOUT, SKAM!
THAT DONALD'S BEEN ON MY TAIL ALL DAY! HOW ABOUT YOU?
THE THREE LITTLE GUYS HAVE BEEN WATCHING ME!

DUCKS! DUCKS! EVERYBODY'S A DUCK!

TAKE IT EASY, KOCKIE! WE HAVE *SOME* PRIVACY! IF WE CAN JUST KEEP OUR "SLUSH FUND" FLOWING TO THE *BOSS—*

? ?

OKAY, I'D SAY WE'VE BEEN RUMBLED!

YEP! BETTER CLEAR OUT!

DRAT! WE'VE SPOOKED 'EM *TOO* WELL! THEY FLED BEFORE WE COULD LEARN ENOUGH!

WHO'S THEIR *BOSS?*

WHO KNOWS? WE'VE GOTTA GO AFTER THEM!

LOOK! THEY'RE TAKING IT ON THE LAM!

WITH ONLY *ONE* SUITCASE BETWEEN THEM! ¿HMM!¿

THEY'LL GET AWAY!

GRAB A TAXI!

THERE *AREN'T* ANY! ONLY *HOTEL LIMOUSINES!*

OH, MY ACHING WALLET!

FOLLOW THAT CAR!

THERE'S A TAXI STAND JUST A FEW BLOCKS OVER—

THERE'S NO TIME TO SWITCH!

WHAT'S THE METER SAY, BOYS? I CAN'T BEAR TO LOOK!

NO METER, BUT HERE'S A RATE SHEET!

$100 AN HOUR?!

WHERE ARE THEY HEADED? OMIGOSH! DISNEYLAND!

HUNDRED DOLLARS... HUNDRED DOLLARS...

Disneyland

‡HEH!‡ WE'LL LOSE 'EM HERE SURE ENOUGH!

ALL WE'VE GOTTA DO IS BLEND IN WITH THE CROWD!

WE'VE BEEN HERE LOADS OF TIMES WITH UNCA MICKEY! THOSE CROOKS CAN'T HIDE IN A PLACE WE KNOW THIS WELL!

BUT—BUT US WITH A LIMO WAITING AT A HUNDRED SMACKERS PER HOUR...

THERE THEY ARE! ON THAT JUNGLE CRUISE BOAT!

⌐HAH!⌐ THEY WON'T GET AWAY THAT EASY!

WAIT, UNCA DONALD!

BACK O' THE LINE, PAL!

NO CUTS!

DON'T CHASE 'EM! IT'S POINTLESS!

YEAH, 'CAUSE THAT BOAT'S GONNA COME RIGHT BACK HERE PRETTY SOON!

QUICK! FOLLOW THAT... UH, OTHER BOAT!

NO PROBLEM! WE'LL BE RIGHT BEHIND 'EM ALL THE WAY!

WOW!

THEY'RE JUMPING OVERBOARD! THAT WON'T DO 'EM ANY GOOD THOUGH!

HEY, YOU! SIT DOWN!

? ? ?

SPLASH

I'LL JUST SWING OVER LIKE DUCKZAN!

WAIT, I DON'T THINK THAT'S ALLOWED—

AHHEEAHHEEAHH!

?? ??
?? ??

SNAP

?

KLONK!

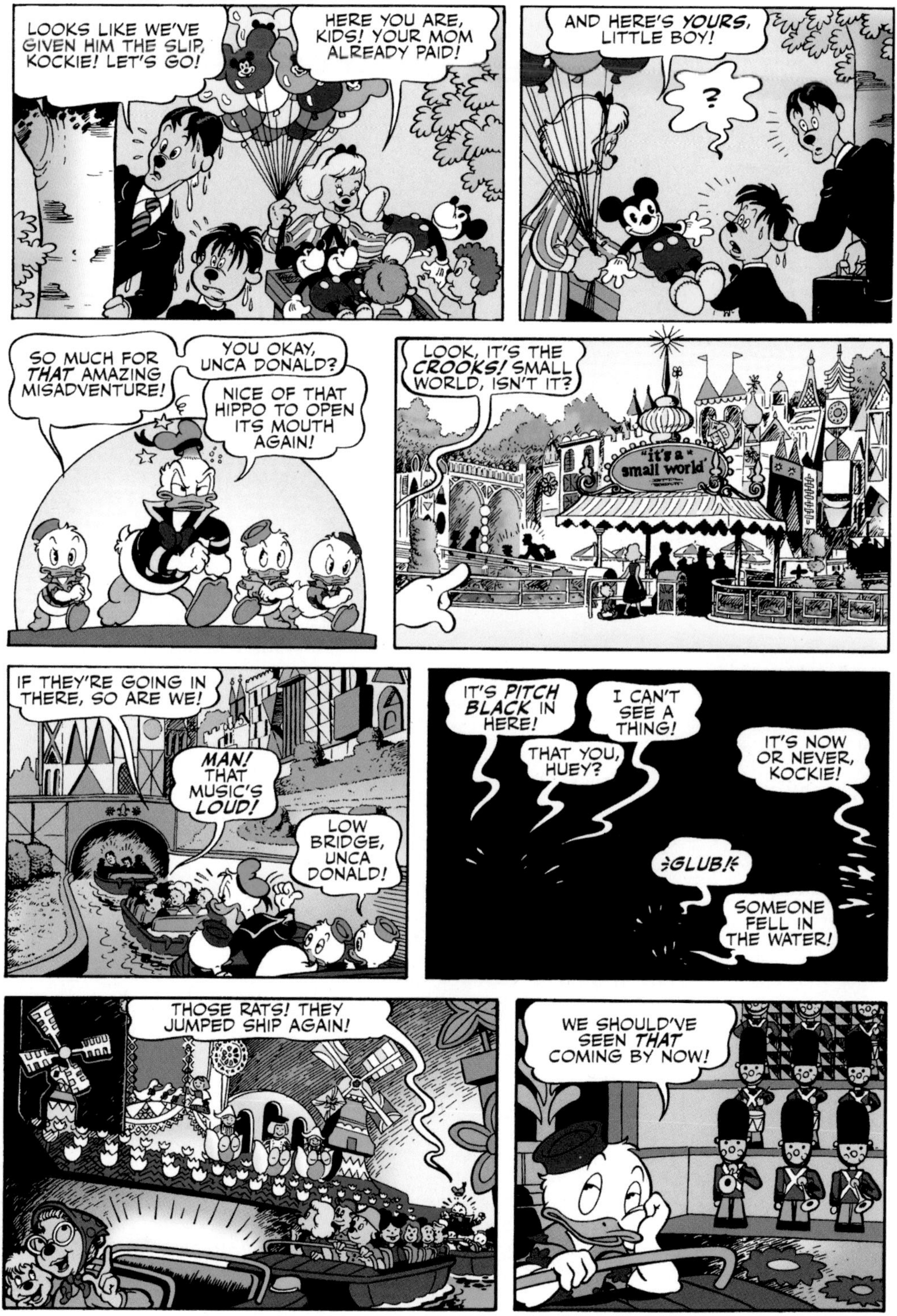

LOOKS LIKE WE'VE GIVEN HIM THE SLIP, KOCKIE! LET'S GO!
HERE YOU ARE, KIDS! YOUR MOM ALREADY PAID!
AND HERE'S YOURS, LITTLE BOY!
?
SO MUCH FOR THAT AMAZING MISADVENTURE!
YOU OKAY, UNCA DONALD?
NICE OF THAT HIPPO TO OPEN ITS MOUTH AGAIN!
LOOK, IT'S THE CROOKS! SMALL WORLD, ISN'T IT?
"it's a small world"
IF THEY'RE GOING IN THERE, SO ARE WE!
MAN! THAT MUSIC'S LOUD!
LOW BRIDGE, UNCA DONALD!
IT'S PITCH BLACK IN HERE!
I CAN'T SEE A THING!
THAT YOU, HUEY?
IT'S NOW OR NEVER, KOCKIE!
GLUB!
SOMEONE FELL IN THE WATER!
THOSE RATS! THEY JUMPED SHIP AGAIN!
WE SHOULD'VE SEEN THAT COMING BY NOW!

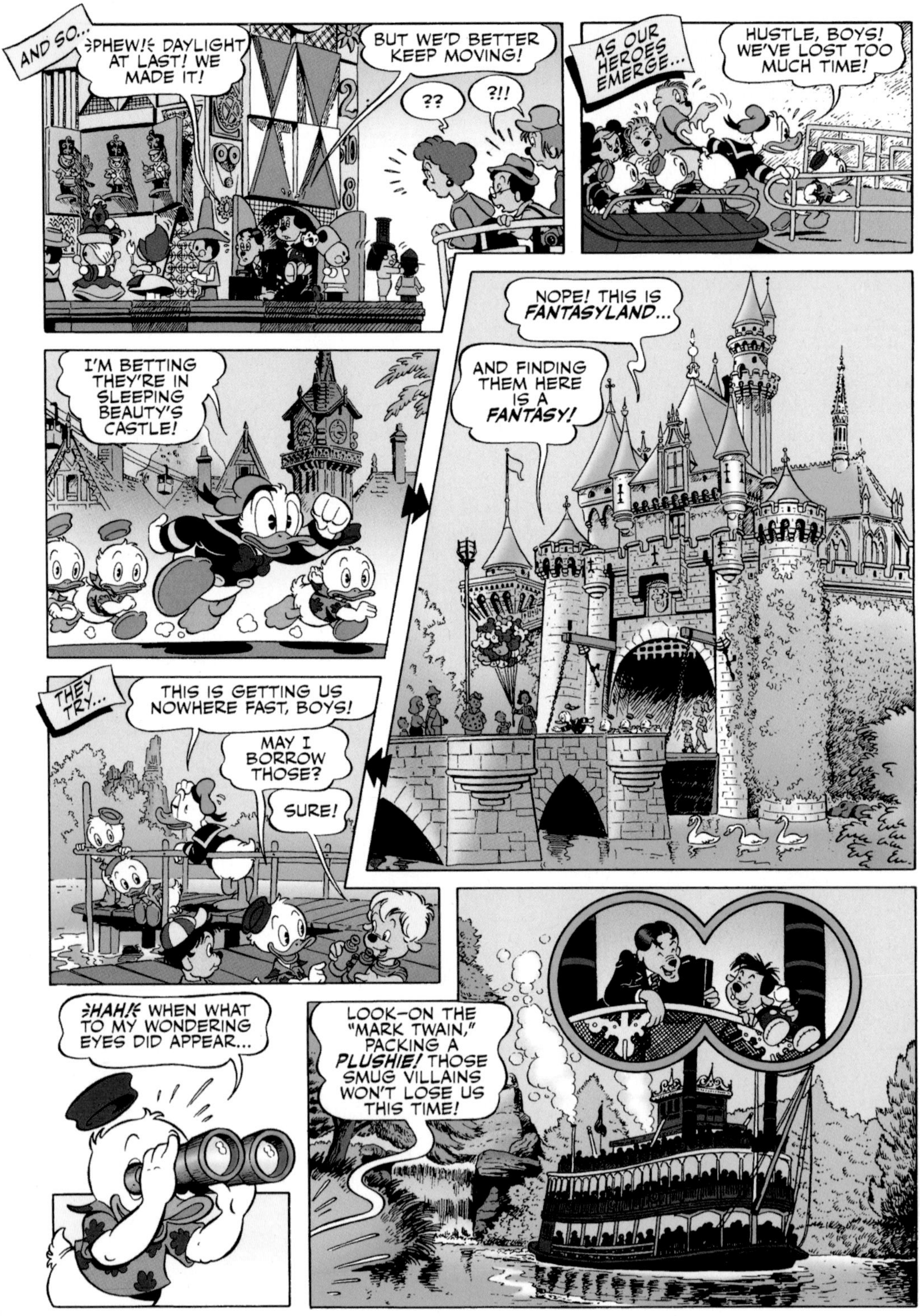

AND SO...
ⲈPHEW!Ⲉ DAYLIGHT AT LAST! WE MADE IT!
BUT WE'D BETTER KEEP MOVING!
??
?!!
AS OUR HEROES EMERGE...
HUSTLE, BOYS! WE'VE LOST TOO MUCH TIME!
I'M BETTING THEY'RE IN SLEEPING BEAUTY'S CASTLE!
NOPE! THIS IS FANTASYLAND...
AND FINDING THEM HERE IS A FANTASY!
THEY TRY...
THIS IS GETTING US NOWHERE FAST, BOYS!
MAY I BORROW THOSE?
SURE!
ⲈHAH!Ⲉ WHEN WHAT TO MY WONDERING EYES DID APPEAR...
LOOK—ON THE "MARK TWAIN," PACKING A PLUSHIE! THOSE SMUG VILLAINS WON'T LOSE US THIS TIME!

C'MON! WE CAN CATCH UP IN THIS BOAT!

DAVY CROCKETT EXPLORER CANOES! NAMED FOR THE MAN WHO *KNEW NO FEAR!*

BUT I'M *AFRAID* OF WATER, JOHN!

TRY TO *KNOW NO FEAR,* MABEL—

CAN'T YOU PADDLE FASTER? WE GOTTA REACH THE "MARK TWAIN"!

THIS AIN'T NO OLYMPIC EVENT, PAL!

THEN *I'LL* TAKE OVER! MOVE ASIDE!

SIT DOWN, UNCA DONALD!

YEAH, YOU IDIOT! WHO PUT YOU IN CHARGE?

SAVE ME, JOHN!

CALM DOWN, OR WE'LL CAPSI—

!!?

SPLASH

THIS JOB WOULD BE A LOT NICER WITHOUT THE TOURISTS!

FOR YOUR INFORMATION, I'M *NOT* ENJOYING THIS!

VERY WISE, OUR UNCA DONALD...

...BEATING A HASTY RETREAT!

MARK TWAIN

LATER...

THOSE DUCKS *MUST'VE* GIVEN UP BY *NOW!*

PIRATES OF THE CARIBBEAN

THIS RIDE WE CAN JUST SIT BACK AND ENJOY!

IT'S MY FAVORITE!

PREPARE TO BOARD YON SCOW, ME HEARTIES!

IT'S *THEM!* WE *CAN'T SHAKE* 'EM!

WATCH OUT, UNCA DONALD!

THAT DOES IT! GOODBYE, DISNEYLAND!

?!!!

?!!!

?!!!

WOOPS!

THAT'S ONE *PUNY* PIRATE!

EEEK!

PLOMP

AND *THAT* WAS ONE *POWERFUL* PUNCH!

ANOTHER HASTY RETREAT!

POW!

ON THE *UPSIDE...* VILLAINS STILL VISIBLE UP AHEAD! ON THE *DOWNSIDE...*

OW... MY EYE!

I THINK I PREFER COMING HERE WHEN WE'RE *RELAXED!*

MEANWHILE ON ANOTHER TRAIL!

BLAIR DUNWITTY? YEP, HE SOLD ME THIS HOUSE SEVERAL YEARS AGO! REAL NICE FELLER!

THEN I'M ON THE RIGHT TRACK!

NERTS!

DO YOU KNOW WHERE HE WENT?

YEAH, *LAS VEGAS!* SAID HE WANTED TO START A FLYING SERVICE!

THANKS! YOU'VE BEEN A BIG HELP!... LAS VEGAS, EH?

AND THERE I'LL TRIP THIS OLD COOT UP FOR *GOOD!*

I'D BETTER GET IN CONTACT WITH MY NEPHEWS!

YOU GO ON, PARTNER! I'VE GOT A FEW THINGS OF MY OWN TO TAKE CARE OF!

FINE BY ME! AND DON'T BOTHER TO KEEP IN TOUCH!

HA, HA! I'LL MISS THAT SENSE OF HUMOR!

ON THE OTHER HAND, DUNWITTY, I'M NOT LETTING *YOU* OUT OF MY *SIGHT!*

ELSEWHERE!

THIS TIME WE'VE LOST THOSE DUCKS FOR *SURE!* I'LL CONTACT THE *BOSS*... HE'LL WANNA *KNOW* WHAT'S GOING ON! UH— NO NEED TO KEEP THAT *TOY.*

AU CONTRAIRE, SKAM! I'VE GOT AN IDEA!

THE PHONE! THAT MUST BE THE BOSS!

GOOD TIMING!

RING!

HELLO! SKAM HERE!

SKAM? IT'S DUNWITTY! McDUCK *WON'T* GIVE UP!... NO, I'M *NOT* SORRY I MADE YOU TAKE THAT HOTEL MANAGER JOB!... JUST MEET ME AT THE WAX MUSEUM, AND BRING THE *YOU-KNOW-WHAT!*

?

OH, *GREAT!* A TRAFFIC JAM!

BUT IT *IS* GREAT, UNCA DONALD! IT'S *HELD BACK* THOSE CROOKS SO WE COULD *FOLLOW* THEM *CLOSER!*

SURE, WHY NOT? IN OUR *$100-PER-HOUR* TAXI...

ONE HOUR LATER!

WE'VE REACHED HOLLYWOOD BOULEVARD!

AND THERE'S THE FAMOUS CHINESE THEATER!

THEY'RE HEADING INTO THE WAX MUSEUM!

BUT THERE'S AN *ENTRANCE FEE!*

THIS HAS BECOME ONE OF THE MOST *EXPENSIVE* FAVORS I'VE EVER DONE FOR THAT OLD SKINFLINT!

THIS *EXCEEDS* YOUR DEAL!

AND HE MIGHT AGREE!

FIRST TIME FOR EVERYTHING, WE GUESS—

LOOK, GUYS! THERE'S A *WAX FIGURE* OF UNCA SCROOGE!

WHAT A LIKENESS! AND SO LIFELIKE!

IT'S THE *REAL ME,* YOU NINNIES! WHAT ARE YOU *DOING* HERE? YOU SHOULD BE AT MY HOTEL TRYING TO FIND OUT WHY IT'S FAILING!

THE *MANAGER'S* WHY... AND HE'S IN *THERE!*

UH-OH! SO'S OWEN DUNWITTY!

AND I'VE GOT A BONE TO PICK WITH YOU, UNK!

OWEN DUNWITTY? WHY WOULD *HE* BE—

WHAT *NOW,* DONALD?

IT'S ABOUT THE EXPENSES I'VE RUN UP BECAUSE OF YOU AND THOSE CROOKS!

WE'D BETTER BUY OUR OWN TICKETS, THEN HAVE A LOOK AROUND!

YEAH! OUR UNCLES ARE *PRE-OCCUPIED!*

...I HAD TO EAT *TOAST* AND *SARDINES...*

YOU THINK *I'D* PAY THOSE PRICES *MYSELF?*

ANOTHER PLUNGE INTO DARKNESS!

I HEAR VOICES OVER THERE! C'MON...

IT'S THEM! WITH DUNWITTY!

SOMETHING TELLS ME THIS IS NO *CHANCE* ENCOUNTER!

IS THIS *ALL* YOU COULD SKIM OFF? I'VE GOT *LOTS* OF CREDIT CARD BILLS TO PAY!

IT'S ALL IN THOUSAND-DOLLAR NOTES, BOSS!

AND EVERY GRAND EARNED! YOUR *SLUSH FUND!*

MEN, IT ALL MAKES SENSE! SKAM USES *CASH* AND *CORPORATE INFO* FROM THE McDUCK OASIS...

TO TURN OWEN INTO A *WEALTHY EXPERT* ON UNCA SCROOGE'S EMPIRE!

SO I CAN SEIZE THE *RIGHT ASSETS* WITH THAT ANCIENT CONTRACT... AND AFFORD TO FIGHT A McDUCK CHALLENGE IN COURT!

YOU'VE *GOT* HIM!

ALMOST! WE STILL MUST MAKE SURE THAT OLD BIRD *NEVER LOCATES* MY DEAR UNCLE BLAIR!

BLAIR DUNWITTY!

SO IT'S TRUE! HE'S STILL *ALIVE!*

BUT WHAT'S WITH THE DISNEY-LAND SOUVENIR?

YOU COULD AT *LEAST* PAY TO GET ME *IN* HERE!

DON'T BOTHER ME WITH DETAILS!

ARE THOSE TWO STILL AT IT?

THEY COULD RUIN EVERYTHING!

RISKING BILLIONS FOR THE SAKE OF A FEW BUCKS!

IT'S THOSE BLASTED *DUCKS!* WE'D BETTER SCRAM!

STUBBORN PESTS!

QUICK! *AFTER* THEM!

HEY!

WHO PUT OUT THE LIGHTS?

UNCA SCROOGE! UNCA DONALD! BLOCK THE EXIT! THEY'RE COMING OUT!

THE EXIT'S OVER HERE... I *THINK!*

I'M PRETTY SURE IT'S OVER *HERE!* ONE OF US OUGHTTA BE RIGHT, ANYWAY!

MY SENSE OF DIRECTION IS INFALLIBLE AND—

AGH!

I GOT ONE! A *BIG* ONE! OWEN DUNWITTY, I BET!

AH! HERE'S THE MAIN POWER SWITCH!

CLICK!

YAAAAAAH!! FRANKENBEAN'S MONSTER!!

HIS PULSE IS OKAY!

THAT'S JUST A *WAX FIGURE,* UNCA SCROOGE!

GASP! IMAGINE IF MY *HEAD* HAD BEEN ON THAT BLOCK!

THE CROOKS ARE GONE! THIS IS GETTING MONOTONOUS!

ANOTHER JOB *NOT* WELL DONE!

THANKS TO OUR UNCLES!

IT WAS *AWFUL!*

HORRID!

I ALMOST LOST MY HEAD BACK THERE!

ALMOST?

SHORTLY!

AT LEAST WE KNOW THOSE THREE GUYS ARE IN COLLUSION!

AND OWEN DUNWITTY'S THE BOSS!

THAT'S FINE, BOYS, BUT...

...WHERE'S THE MONEY THEY TOOK FROM THE HOTEL?

THEY HAD...

A *SUITCASE,* BUT...

MAYBE...

OKAY, WE'LL DEAL WITH THAT LATER! RIGHT NOW WE'VE GOT TO GET BACK ON *BLAIR* DUNWITTY'S TRAIL!

WHAT DID YOU FIND OUT, UNCA SCROOGE?

THAT WE'RE HOPPING THE NEXT FLIGHT TO LAS VEGAS! *TAXI!*

YOU'RE PAYING FOR *ALL* OUR TICKETS, I PRESUME?

HOW CAN I? MY WALLET'S EMPTY!

AND MINE *ISN'T?!*

MEANWHILE, OVER LOS ANGELES...

THOSE DUCKS WILL BE HEADING TO VEGAS TOO, BUT WE GOT THE *JUMP* ON 'EM!

HEE-HEE!

SURE ENOUGH, ONCE THERE...

HURRY, BOYS! EVERY *MILLISECOND* COUNTS!

ANY CHANCE WE'LL EVER REACH THE *END* OF THIS MARATHON?

YOUNG MAN! CAN YOU TELL ME IF THIS IS BLAIR DUNWITTY'S AIRLINE?

IT *WAS*, BUT THAT WAS A WHILE AGO!

HE *SOLD* IT AND *TOOK OFF*!

CAN YOU TELL ME WHERE? IT'S IMPORTANT!

HE SAID HE WAS MOVING TO THE *GRAND CANYON*!

THEN THAT'S WHERE *WE* NEED TO GO! I'LL TAKE FIVE ROUND-TRIP TICKETS!

WISH I COULD OBLIGE, BUT THREE OTHER GUYS RENTED *ALL THE PLANES*! FOR *CASH*!

WHAAAT?

YEP! THERE THEY GO!

BLAST!

RRRRRRRRRRR

IT'S THEIR DARN *SLUSH FUND* MONEY AGAIN!

UNCA SCROOGE, SAY SOMETHING! WE...

...HATE TO SEE YOU...

...LIKE THIS!

BWAAH!

BLUBBING'S NOT WHAT WE MEANT!

WAAAH!

SHEESH! GETTING HYSTERICAL'S NOT GONNA HELP!

ME? HYSTERICAL?! HOW CALM WERE *YOU* IN THE WAX MUSEUM?

SCARED WITLESS, SURE—BUT ONLY THANKS TO *YOUR* DRAMA!

MY DRAMA?! TSK... INSULTING THE UNCLE WHO PAID FOR YOUR ROOF REPAIRS LAST MONTH!

YOU *LOANED* ME THE MONEY AT *48%* *INTEREST!* THAT SCARED ME WITLESS *TOO*—

VRROOOM!

? ?

VRROOOOM!

BLESS MY BAGPIPES! A PLANE'S LANDING!

RICH GUY LUCK AGAIN!

MISS! CAN YOU FLY US TO THE GRAND CANYON?

NAME'S MARY, AND I CAN! HOP IN!

YOU'RE AN *ANGEL*, MARY! A TREASURE, A JEWEL, A—

DIAL IT DOWN, UNCLE SCROOGE!

ONCE AT THE CANYON, WE SHOULD FIND BLAIR IN NO TIME!

BLAIR? *BLAIR DUNWITTY?*

THAT'S RIGHT! DO YOU KNOW HIM?

SURE I DO! *ALL* US REGIONAL PILOTS DO! GREAT GUY!

HE RAN ONE OF THE BEST AIR SERVICES AROUND! AND SO *GENEROUS!* WE ALL LIKED HIM, BUT ONE DAY...

YEAH? WHAT HAPPENED?

HE GOT INTO ONE OF HIS PLANES AND *DISAPPEARED* INTO THE CANYON!

DISAPPEARED? THAT'S IT?

HE ONCE SAID HE WAS *TIRED* OF THE CIVILIZED WORLD, AND WANTED TO FIND *PEACE!* THE GRAND CANYON WAS HIS IDEA OF *PARADISE!*

PEACE AND PARADISE, EH? THAT FIGURES.

I COULD SURE USE A HEAPING HELPING OF *BOTH* RIGHT NOW...

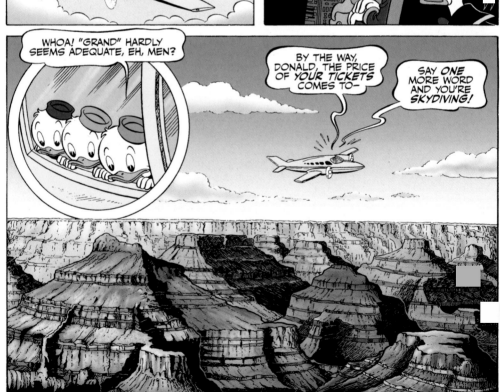

WHOA! "GRAND" HARDLY SEEMS ADEQUATE, EH, MEN?

BY THE WAY, DONALD, THE PRICE OF *YOUR TICKETS* COMES TO—

SAY *ONE* MORE WORD AND YOU'RE *SKYDIVING!*

G'BYE, MARY, AND THANKS!

GOOD LUCK, GANG!

LET'S START AT THAT *MOTEL!* SOMEONE THERE MIGHT KNOW WHERE BLAIR IS!

THEY *MIGHT* NOT EVEN ASK FOR A *TIP!*

Worst Western

SURE! I KNOW BLAIR DUNWITTY, BUT I HAVEN'T SEEN HIM IN SOME TIME!

AND YOU HAVE NO IDEA WHERE HE *MIGHT* BE?

THE GRAND CANYON'S *450* MILES LONG... WITH A ZILLION SIDE CANYONS! HE COULD BE *ANYWHERE!*

NOW, BOYS, DON'T TROUBLE UNCLE SCROOGE WITH *MINOR* DETAILS LIKE THAT!

MAYBE YOU COULD RENT A CAR AND CHECK THINGS OUT FROM THE RIM. THAT'S WHAT I ADVISED THOSE *OTHER* THREE GUYS TO DO!

OTHER THREE? WHAT DID THEY LOOK LIKE?

TWO TALL MEN, ONE WITH A SUITCASE... ONE SHORT GUY WITH A STUFFED TOY!

THAT'S THEM!

MY *MONEY'S* IN DANGER! AND *BLAIR* TOO!

SORRY, ALL MY VEHICLES HAVE BEEN RENTED!

AAARGH!

STORY OF OUR LIVES!

CLEM'S CARS 'N' CATTLE

YOU MIGHT TRY RENTIN' A *BOAT!*

A BOAT? *WHERE? TELL* ME! IT'S A MATTER OF *LIFE* AND *DEBT!*

NO BOATS LEFT, FELLAS! *SORRY!*

SO ARE *WE!*

NOW WHAT?

SOME-BODY THINK OF SOME-THING!

McSHOAT'S BOATS

ANYONE GOT ANY *BRIGHT* IDEAS?

-:HMPH!:- NOT ME!

HEY! THAT'S *IT!*

WE'LL BORROW *THIS* BOAT!

YOU SURE, UNCA SCROOGE?

IT'S A *MUSEUM DISPLAY,* NOT AN *ACTUAL* RIVERBOAT!

IT'S AN AUTHENTIC REPLICA! IT'LL DO THE JOB!

AH, BUT HOW'LL YOU GET IT *DOWN* TO THE COLORADO?

?

I'LL GIVE THOSE KIDS A *DIME* FOR SKATE RENTAL WHEN WE GET BACK!

I'M NOT SURE THEY'LL SEE THAT AS A SATISFACTORY TRANSACTION!

HELP! MURDER! *POLICE!*

WE JUST PASSED THE TRAILHEAD, UNCA SCROOGE!

I KNOW! GOING DOWN *TRAILS* WILL TAKE TOO *LONG!*

THEN HOW...WAIT, YOU DON'T MEAN—

NEARBY!

SACRE BLEU! MY *BEST* LANDSCAPE YET! I FEEL LIKE ZE VERITABLE *LADY REMBRANDT!*

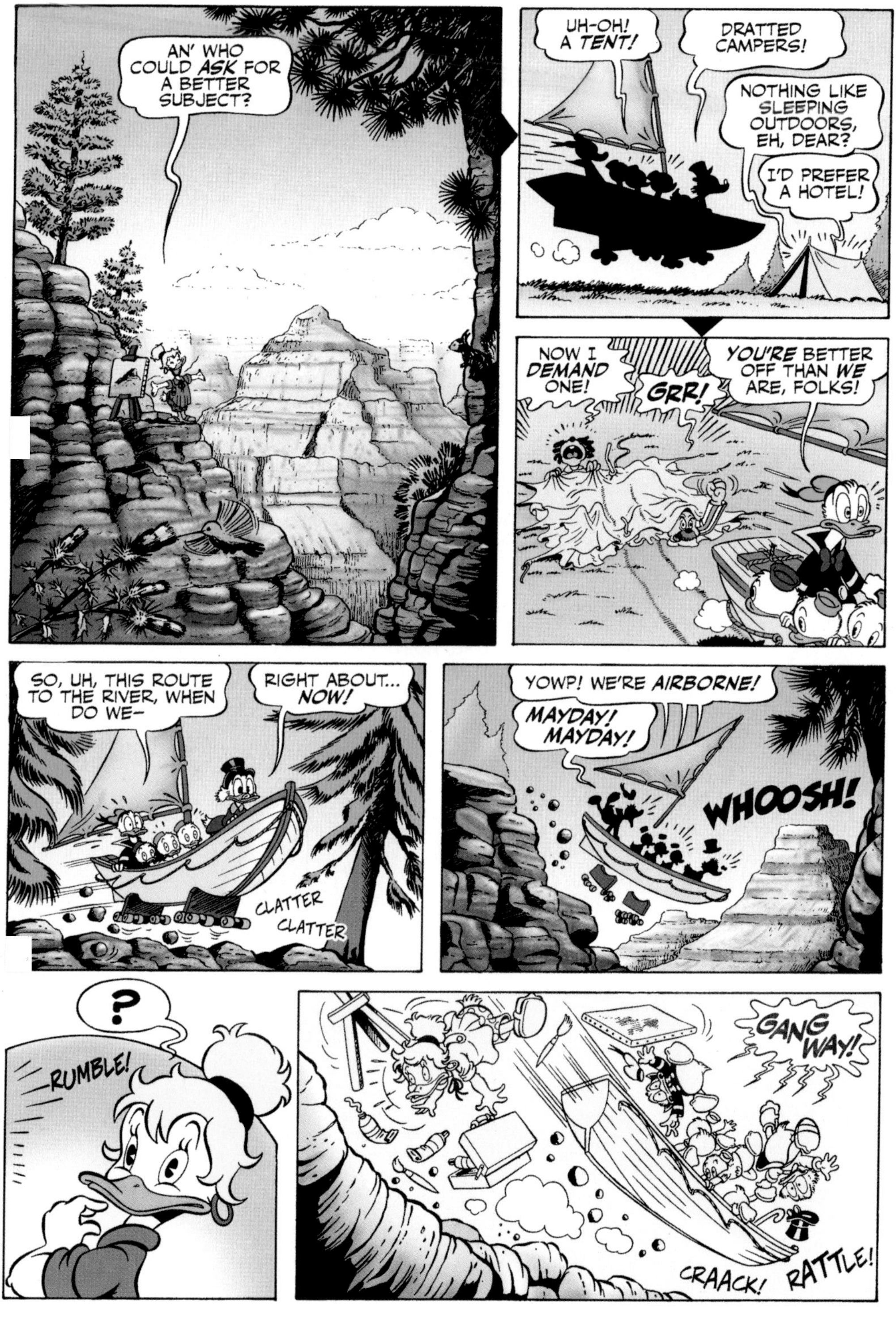
AN' WHO COULD ASK FOR A BETTER SUBJECT?
UH-OH! A TENT!
DRATTED CAMPERS!
NOTHING LIKE SLEEPING OUTDOORS, EH, DEAR?
I'D PREFER A HOTEL!
NOW I DEMAND ONE!
GRR!
YOU'RE BETTER OFF THAN WE ARE, FOLKS!
SO, UH, THIS ROUTE TO THE RIVER, WHEN DO WE–
RIGHT ABOUT... NOW!
CLATTER
CLATTER
YOWP! WE'RE AIRBORNE!
MAYDAY! MAYDAY!
WHOOSH!
?
RUMBLE!
GANG WAY!
CRAACK!
RATTLE!

?!

KAROOM!

YOU HEAR *THUNDER*, OTTO?

YEAH, BUT THERE ARE NO CLOUDS!

MAYBE IT'S ECHOING DOWN TH—

BAROOM!

YEEEEOW!!!

FWISSH

SPLASH!

THERE! FROM THE RIM TO THE RIVER IN NO TIME FLAT! I *KNEW* IT WOULD WORK!

IT *DID*, DID IT?

ARE WE STILL IN ONE PIECE?

B-BUMP

B-BUMP!

HMM... WE *MIGHT* WANNA RETURN BY *ANOTHER* ROUTE!

NEVER MIND THOSE IDLERS! DONALD, TAKE THE HELM!

OKAY, BUT THAT MEANS I'M ON THE CLOCK!

FINE! I JUST HOPE WE FIND BLAIR BEFORE THOSE CROOKS DO!

HEY, EVERYBODY! *LOOK!*

THERE THEY *ARE!*

AND WE'RE *TOO LATE!* THEY ALREADY HAVE HIM!

HEAD FOR THAT SANDBAR, DONALD! *HURRY!*

WHADDAYA *THINK* I'M DOING?

DARN! WE'VE GONE *PAST* IT!

WE CAN'T LOSE SIGHT OF THOSE MUGS AGAIN! TURN AROUND! *TURN AROUND!*

AGAINST *THIS* CURRENT? DREAM ON!

WHAT NOW, GREAT LEADER?

WE'LL HAVE TO LAND! TAKE A HARD RIGHT!

NOT *THAT* HARD!

CRACK!

TIE US UP, AND THEN EVERYBODY ASHORE!

WHACK!

HURRY! TIME'S A-WASTIN'!

JUST HOLD YOUR HORSES!

OKAY! LET'S GO!

I THOUGHT I'D *LOST* MY OLD AGREEMENT WITH SCROOGE McDUCK! AND YOU *FOUND* IT IN MY KID BROTHER'S *MEMENTO CHEST?!*

YOUR *LATE* KID BROTHER, UNK...

...WHO'D BE *SORRY* HE ADOPTED A SON LIKE ME!

NOW, UNK! I JUST NEED TO *HIDE* YOU FOR A BIT, ON—SAY...

...THE ISLAND OF SANTA ROSA!

BUT A SUPPLY SHIP ARRIVES THERE EVERY TWO MONTHS. I'LL JUST TAKE THAT *BACK*—UNLESS YOU AIM TO STOP ME!

WHY WOULD I? TWO MONTHS IS ALL I'LL NEED TO *RUIN* SCROOGE McDUCK!

YOU *BOUNDER!*

OWEN DUNWITTY WON'T ESCAPE ME THIS TIME!

I HATE TO SAY IT, UNCA SCROOGE, BUT...

...HE *ALREADY HAS!*

SEE THAT CANOE?

DRAT! BLAST AND DRAT!

LOOKS LIKE HE'S HAD THE LAST LAUGH!

NOT ON *ME* HE HASN'T! THAT'S BLAIR'S OLD PLANE OVER THERE, DONALD! TAKE IT UP AND FOLLOW THEM!

BUT I'VE NEVER FLOWN THAT TYPE!

OH, NEVER MIND! I'LL FIGURE IT OUT!

JUST HOPE I DON'T CRASH AND BURN IN THE PROCESS!

CLICK!

BLAIR DUNWITTY HERE! THE FOLLOWING ARE THE OPERATING SPECIFICS AND *CHECKLIST* FOR THIS MODEL...

ALL *RIGHT!* A RECORDED TUTORIAL!

...AND PAY PARTICULAR ATTENTION TO THE OIL PRESSURE...

CHECK, MR. DUNWITTY!

...BECAUSE IT COULD *PLUNGE UNEXPECTEDLY...*

WHAT?

...AND CAUSE IMMEDIATE ENGINE FAILURE...

YIKES!

AGH! THERE IT GOES! AND HERE *I* GO!

TUNK! TUNK! TUNK!

C'MON, THE HELICOPTER'S WAITING!

IF I CAN JUST *LOOSEN* THIS ROPE...

RRRRRRRrrrrR!

EH? WHAT'S THAT?

?

-HEH!- I KNOW EXACTLY!

VAMOOSE, GUYS! THAT *PILOT* MUST BE A *LUNATIC!*

GOTTA TIME THIS JUST RIGHT...

RRRRRRRRR

CRACK!

ROPED 'IM!

SO LONG! IT'S BEEN FUN!

UH-OH, I'VE SNAGGED SOMETHING!

HE *GOT AWAY!* I'M BETTING IT WAS THOSE LOUSY *DUCKS!*

THE HELICOPTER'S WRECKED!

BUT WE STILL HAVE THE CANOE!

I'M A *WELL-TRAVELED* OLD BIRD, BUT I'VE NEVER FLOWN LIKE *THIS!*

I FOUND THE CROOKS! NOW FOR A PLACE TO LAND!

ECONOMY CLASS IS GETTING *RIDICULOUS!*

PLUS THE DO-RE-MI FROM THE HOTEL! LET'S GET BACK TO VEGAS!

AND DO WHAT? *GAMBLE?*

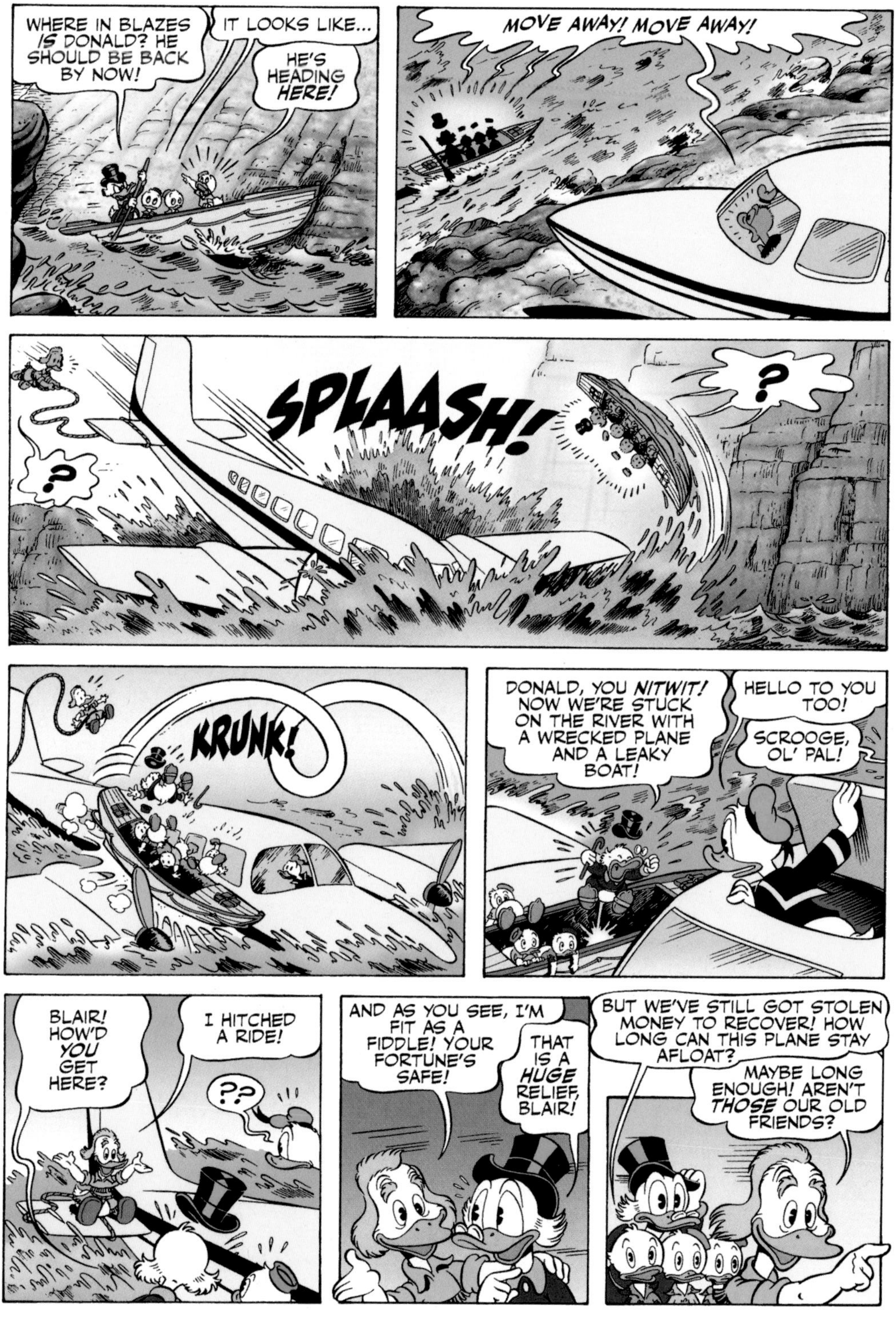
WHERE IN BLAZES *IS* DONALD? HE SHOULD BE BACK BY NOW!
IT LOOKS LIKE...
HE'S HEADING *HERE!*
MOVE AWAY! MOVE AWAY!
SPLAASH!
?
?
KRUNK!
DONALD, YOU *NITWIT!* NOW WE'RE STUCK ON THE RIVER WITH A WRECKED PLANE AND A LEAKY BOAT!
HELLO TO YOU TOO!
SCROOGE, OL' PAL!
BLAIR! HOW'D *YOU* GET HERE?
I HITCHED A RIDE!
??
AND AS YOU SEE, I'M FIT AS A FIDDLE! YOUR FORTUNE'S SAFE!
THAT IS A *HUGE* RELIEF, BLAIR!
BUT WE'VE STILL GOT STOLEN MONEY TO RECOVER! HOW LONG CAN THIS PLANE STAY AFLOAT?
MAYBE LONG ENOUGH! AREN'T *THOSE* OUR OLD FRIENDS?

YEP, AND THEY'RE *GETTING AWAY* AGAIN! THEY'RE SLIPPERIER THAN A *CANYONFUL* OF EELS!

YOU'D LIKE THAT SUITCASE BACK THOUGH, EH?

I MIGHT BE ABLE TO HELP YOU THERE!

WHAT DO YOU HAVE IN MIND?

I USED TO BE A *CHAMPION ROPER*, REMEMBER? AND I STILL HAVE THE CHOPS!

GONNA TRY TO *LASSO* US OUTTA HERE?

NOTHING THAT AMBITIOUS! IT'S GONNA BE TRICKY, BUT...

...I'LL GIVE IT A TRY!

HAH! JUST LIKE THE OLD DAYS!

WHIZZZ!

TOSSING A LASSO FROM A *FLOATING PLANE!* WHAT NEXT?

YEE-HAH! DEAD ON TARGET!

ZZZIP!

??!

?

SNAP!!

NOOO! NOT OUR *DISNEYLAND SOUVENIR!*

WHAT THE HEY?

WHY ARE YOU WORRIED ABOUT A *TOY?*

I GET THE FEELING THERE'S SOMETHING YOU'RE *NOT* TELLING ME!

≳GULP!≲

GUESS MY AIM'S NOT WHAT IT USED TO BE!

THAT WAS *STILL* AN AMAZING THROW, BLAIR!

OH, WOE! ALL THAT EMBEZZLED CASH... *GONE!* ≳SOB!≲

THERE THEY GO, INTO THAT SIDE CANYON! WE *WON'T* BE ABLE TO FOLLOW, AND... FACT IS, WE DON'T *WANT* TO!

Y'MEAN WE MIGHT *NEVER* COME OUT?

NO ONE *EVER* HAS! BUT THAT'S NOT OUR WORRY! MY OLD EARS ARE PICKING UP THE ROAR OF THE WATERFALL!

WATERFALL? HOW FAR IS IT?

≳ULP!≲ ASK A SILLY QUESTION!

IF ONLY THIS WERE A *DISNEYLAND WATERSLIDE!*

RUMMBLE!

ALL FOR A SUITCASE FULL OF MONEY WE'LL *NEVER* RECOVER!

SUMS IT UP, I'D SAY!

WITH *GUSTO!*

OH, THE *TRAGEDY!* BWAAH!

AT LEAST WE GOT TO MEET AGAIN, OLD PARTNER! I, FOR ONE, AM CONTENT!

HE REALLY IS A SWEET GUY!

I CAN'T *BEAR* TO LOOK—

KRUCK! CRACK!

WHADDAYA KNOW! WE'RE *STUCK!*

HOT DOG! THE WINGS GOT JAMMED BEHIND THOSE ROCKS!

YIPPEEEE!!

BWAAH!

RUMMBLE

WE'D BETTER GET OFF THE PLANE WHILE WE CAN!

ARE THEY SHOOTING A *DISASTER* FILM?

MAYBE! THAT'S ONE PRETTY *CRAZY* STUNT!

WILL YOU STOP BAWLING? THAT MONEY'S GONE... GET OVER IT!

YOU'D BE JUST AS BROKEN UP IF *YOU'D* LOST IT!

WE'VE BEEN THINKING ABOUT THAT!

IT'S POSSIBLE THAT SUIT-CASE WAS EMPTY!

WHAT DID YOU SAY?

SKAM AND THE SERVER WERE ACTING KINDA ODD!

LIKE THEY *WEREN'T* THAT *CONCERNED* ABOUT THE SUITCASE!

WAAAAAAH!

Y'MEAN THERE WAS *NO MONEY?* WE CHASED 'EM FOR *NOTHING?*

WE'RE NOT SAYING THERE WAS NO MONEY! WE'RE JUST *WONDERING* IF MAYBE IT WAS SOMEWHERE *ELSE!*

LET'S SEE IF WE'RE RIGHT!

VOILA! IT WAS TAKEN OUT OF THE SUITCASE AND STUFFED INTO—

CUSHLA-MACREE!

MY *MONEY!* MY DARLING, BEAUTIFUL, PRECIOUS, RADIANT, DEARLY BELOVED *MONEY!* COME TO PAPA!

REUNIONS LIKE THIS ARE ALWAYS SO HEARTWARMING!

NEXT DAY, AT THE CANYON MUSEUM!

THAT REPLICA'S *EXTRA* AUTHENTIC NOW!

A NICE REMINDER...

...FOR US!

SCROOGE!

MERCEDES PUJOL! FANCY MEETING YOU HERE!

I'M ON HOLIDAY AN' PAINTING UP A STORM! CARE TO SEE?

I'M PLANNING TO EXHIBIT IN BARCELONA!

GUESS YOU WON'T BE SHOWING *THAT* ONE! WHAT *HAPPENED?*

IT WAS ONE OF MY BEST, BUT GOT RUINED BY ZIS BUNCH OF *HOOLIGANS* IN A *BOAT!* ON *LAND,* IF YOU CAN BELIEVE IT!

SUCH... A... SHAME... ABOUT... THAT!

HAVE YOU *THOUGHT* ABOUT IT, BLAIR?

YUP! I'M STAYING HERE! YOU'RE THE BUSINESSMAN, I'D JUST GET IN THE WAY!

WELL, THEN—*GOOD LUCK!* AND THANKS FOR THIS *RELEASE* GIVING ME *FULL CONTROL* OVER MY FORTUNE!

OKAY, THAT'S SETTLED! CAN WE GO *HOME* NOW?

SCHOOL'S STARTING!

NOT UNTIL NEXT WEEK! YOU LADS DESERVE A *REAL* VACATION, AND THE McDUCK OASIS NEEDS THE *BUSINESS!*

HOORAY!

ALL EXPENSES PAID BY *YOU* THIS TIME?

OF COURSE! WHY NOT?

YOU HEARD THAT WITH YOUR OWN EARS, BOYS! LET'S GO!

SNAP!

IMAGINE! UNCA SCROOGE DECIDED TO RUN THE HOTEL *PERSONALLY!*

HE'LL *HAVE* TO, UNTIL HE FINDS A MANAGER HE CAN *TRUST!*

AND A *SERVER* HE CAN TRUST, TOO!

SORRY, DONALD, BUT *SOMEONE* HAS TO COVER THE BEVERAGE DETAIL! NOW *MOVE ALONG* BEFORE THE ICE CREAM IN THAT ROOT BEER FLOAT MELTS!

ALL'S WELL THAT ENDS WELL... (?)

Walt Disney's GYRO GEARLOOSE

GYRO! I'M *DESPERATE*... I NEED YOUR *INVENTIVE HELP!*

AWK! WATCH IT! THERE'S FRAGILE EQUIPMENT IN HERE!

I'M TRYING TO SET A NEW RECORD FOR *POLE-SITTING,* BUT I CAN'T CLIMB THIS POLE WITHOUT GETTING *SCARED* OF *HEIGHTS!*

HAVE YOU CONSIDERED A NEW HOBBY?

...NEVER MIND!... TO *HELP* YOU, I MUST DETERMINE *EXACTLY WHEN* YOUR FEAR SETS IN!

STAND ON THIS CHAIR AND LET ME KNOW HOW YOU FEEL!

HEY, PIECE OF CAKE!

HMM... LOOKS LIKE WE'LL HAVE TO GO HIGHER!

I'LL HOIST YOU UP, AND YOU HOLLER WHEN YOU START FEELING SCARED!

SO FAR, SO GOOD!

≳*AAAH!*≲ LET ME DOWN! *HALP!*

GOT IT! TERROR STRIKES AT 21 FEET, 4½ INCHES!

YOUR *POLE* HOLDS YOU A FEW INCHES *HIGHER* THAN THAT... SO WE *TAKE OFF* A FEW INCHES AND YOU'RE SET!

THAT'S *IT?* SIMPLE! I COULD HAVE DONE *THAT* AT HOME!

AND HERE I WAS EXPECTING AN ACTUAL *INVENTION!* PFFT!

⸘OOF!⸱ GLAD TO BE OF SERVICE!

⸘UGH!⸱ OF COURSE THE PROBLEM SEEMS *SIMPLE* ONCE IT'S *SOLVED!* CUSTOMERS CAN BE SO UNGRATEFUL!

THAT'S *SO* TRUE!

BUT IF YOU HELP *ME,* I'LL BE *ETERNALLY* GRATEFUL!

THAT'S GREAT! HOW *CAN* I HELP YOU, MA'AM?

I WANT TO BE *TALLER!*

TALLER? BUT YOU'RE ALREADY ALMOST AS TALL AS I AM!

SO? I'M THE CUSTOMER, AND *I'M* SAYING I WANT TO BE *TALLER!*

IF YOU CAN'T HELP ME, I'LL TAKE MY BUSINESS—

I CAN HELP YOU! JUST TAKE OFF YOUR SHOES!

LUCKY I HELD ONTO THIS SPARE PIECE OF *PIPE!*

NEVER KNOW WHEN I'LL FIND USES FOR THINGS! I'LL JUST CUT IT DOWN...

...ADD A DROP OF *GEARGLUE,* AND VOILA! THE PERFECT *HEELS!*

HEELS? NOW I SEE WHY YOUR CUSTOMERS ARE UNGRATEFUL!

I SOLVED YOUR PROBLEM—BUT IT'S *STILL* NOT GOOD ENOUGH! YOU WANT TO BE TALLER?

I'LL *GIVE* YOU TALLER!

I'LL *WAIT.*

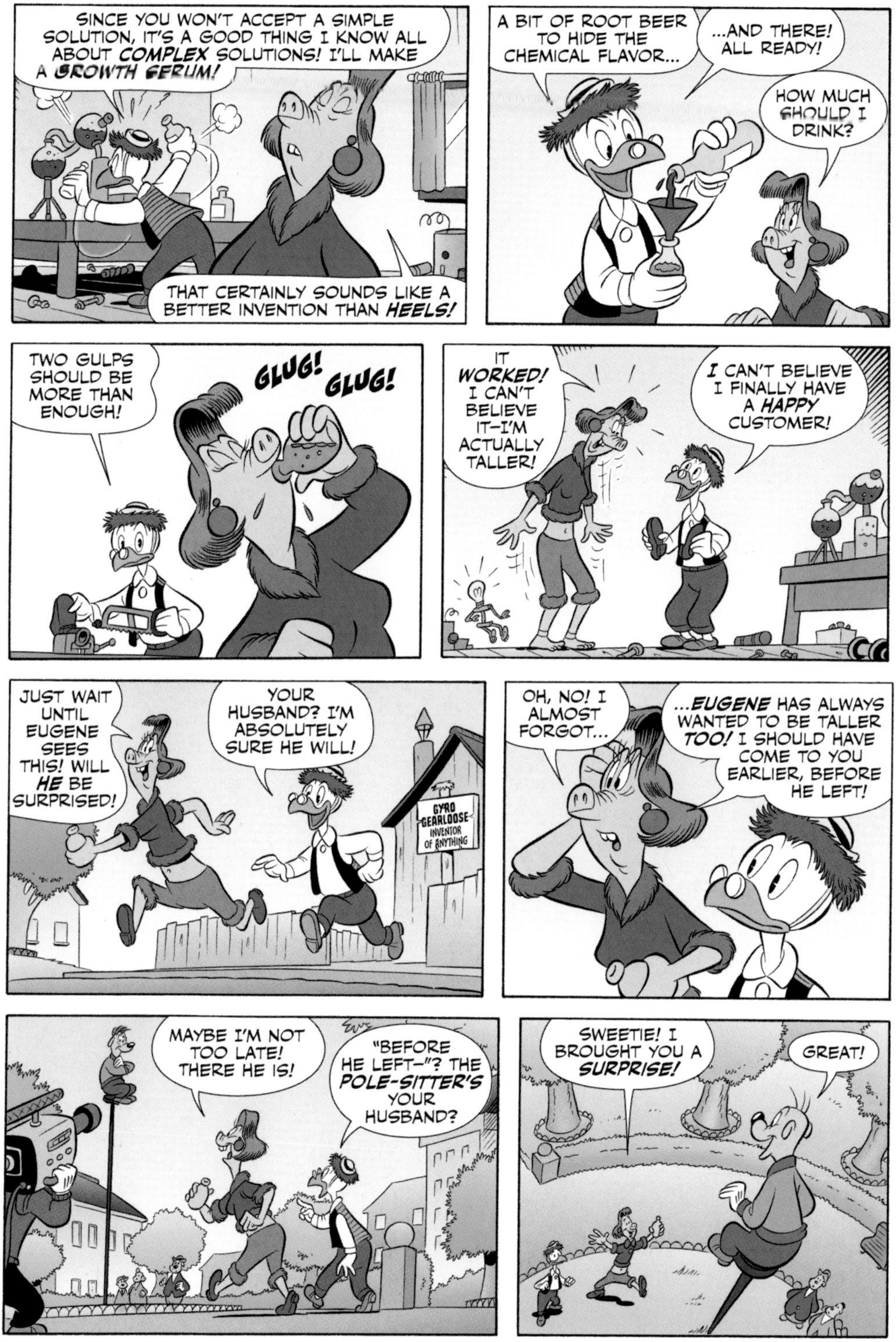
SINCE YOU WON'T ACCEPT A SIMPLE SOLUTION, IT'S A GOOD THING I KNOW ALL ABOUT *COMPLEX* SOLUTIONS! I'LL MAKE A *GROWTH SERUM!*
THAT CERTAINLY SOUNDS LIKE A BETTER INVENTION THAN *HEELS!*
A BIT OF ROOT BEER TO HIDE THE CHEMICAL FLAVOR...
...AND THERE! ALL READY!
HOW MUCH SHOULD I DRINK?
TWO GULPS SHOULD BE MORE THAN ENOUGH!
GLUG! GLUG!
IT *WORKED!* I CAN'T BELIEVE IT—I'M ACTUALLY TALLER!
I CAN'T BELIEVE I FINALLY HAVE A *HAPPY* CUSTOMER!
JUST WAIT UNTIL EUGENE SEES THIS! WILL *HE* BE SURPRISED!
YOUR HUSBAND? I'M ABSOLUTELY SURE HE WILL!
GYRO GEARLOOSE INVENTOR OF ANYTHING
OH, NO! I ALMOST FORGOT...
...*EUGENE* HAS ALWAYS WANTED TO BE TALLER *TOO!* I SHOULD HAVE COME TO YOU EARLIER, BEFORE HE LEFT!
MAYBE I'M NOT TOO LATE! THERE HE IS!
"BEFORE HE LEFT—"? THE *POLE-SITTER'S* YOUR HUSBAND?
SWEETIE! I BROUGHT YOU A *SURPRISE!*
GREAT!

IT'S A DREAM COME TRUE, EUGENE! HERE, DRINK THIS SERUM GYRO MADE!

I DON'T KNOW ABOUT A *SERUM*, BUT I SURE COULD USE A REFRESHING DRINK!

GLUG!

GLUG!

GLUG!

NOT TOO MUCH, DEAR! IT'S VERY POTENT!

WE'VE HEARD THAT *YOU* HELPED OUR HERO PREPARE FOR HIS RECORD-BREAKING FEAT TODAY! DID YOU INVENT SPECIAL POLE-SITTING CLOTHES?

NOPE! JUST MADE A SIMPLE *CALCULATION!*

ALL I HAD TO DO WAS DETERMINE THE HEIGHT AT WHICH EUGENE'S VESTIBULAR SYSTEM TRIGGERED HIS ACROPHOBIA!

-:HEH!:- ONE MORE TIME IN *ENGLISH*, MR. GEARLOOSE?

SURE! TO THE INCH—THE *EXACT HEIGHT* WHERE HE BECOMES *AFRAID OF HEIGHTS!*

GROW!

AGH!

HEEALLP! SOMEBODY GET ME DOWN FROM HERE!

THIS IS ALL *YOUR* FAULT!

RUIN MY *RECORD* ATTEMPT, EH?

AWK! I GUESS YOU REALLY *CAN'T* PLEASE EVERYONE AFTER ALL!

End!

WALT DISNEY'S UNCLE $CROOGE in
BELLE CORNERS THE COIN COLLECTION

AN *1803 HALF-DRUBNIK!* ¿DROOL!¿ THE *ONLY* COIN MISSING FROM MY 19TH CENTURY COLLECTION!

YES, MR. McDUCK! I *KNEW* YOU'D BE INTERESTED IN BUYING IT!

YOU'LL SELL IT TO ME? YOU *MUST!*

OF COURSE... FOR $10,000!

$10,000! HIGHWAY *ROBBERY!*

TAKE IT OR LEAVE IT, MR. McDUCK!

THIS IS THE *ONLY* 1803 HALF-DRUBNIK YOU MAY *EVER* SEE!

I KNOW! I'LL TAKE IT! I'LL TAKE IT!

TEN THOUSAND DOLLARS FOR *ONE* OLD COIN! BUT IT'S *WORTH* IT! THERE HASN'T BEEN AN 1803 HALF-DRUBNIK ON THE MARKET IN 40 YEARS!

LATER... BACK HOME!

MY 19TH CENTURY COLLECTION IS COMPLETE! NOW I CAN—

HAA-HA!

WATCH OUT!

NOW WHAT ARE THOSE KIDS UP TO?

HEY! THIS IS FUN!

IT'S MY TURN!

AWK!

WHEEE!

HURRY UP!

I'M NEXT!

WHAT DO YOU BRATS THINK YOU'RE DOING?!

WE WERE JUST...

...PLAY-ING IN YOUR

...MO-NEY, UNCA SCR-OOGE!

PLAY IN MY BEAUTIFUL MONEY? UNBELIEVABLE!

BUT YOU SWIM IN IT!

AND YOU CAN'T NOT USE IT...

...FOR ANYTHING ELSE!

MONEY IS FOR LOOKING AT! AND TOUCHING! AND KEEPING! NOW RAKE THOSE BILLS SMOOTH AND GET THAT SLED OUT OF HERE!

YES, UNCA SCROOGE!

SWIMMING IS *GENTLE ARTISTRY!* SLEDDING IS *ROUGH FUN!* NEVER AGAIN, OR—

SOMEONE'S AT THE DOOR, UNCA SCROOGE!

NOK NOK

YES? WHAT IS IT?

TELEGRAM FOR SCROOGE McDUCK!

THAT WAS VERY FINE OF YOU TO BRING IT ALL THE WAY OUT HERE! HERE'S A GENEROUS REWARD FOR YOUR SERVICE!

GEE, *THANKS!*

A WHOLE PENNY! MR. McDUCK GAVE ME A *WHOLE PENNY!*... WOW, WHAT A *CHEAPSKATE.*

MY STARS! IT'S FROM *BELLE DUCK!* SHE'S COMING TO VISIT US!

BELLE DUCK?

WHO'S BELLE DUCK, UNCA SCROOGE?

WE NEVER HEARD OF HER!

MISS BELLE IS NEARLY THE *SWEETEST* LITTLE LADY IN THE WHOLE WORLD! I HAVEN'T SEEN HER IN *40* YEARS, BUT I REMEMBER HER AS IF IT WAS YESTERDAY!

SHE'S SO GENTLE... SO REFINED! BE ON YOUR *BEST* BEHAVIOR WHILE SHE'S HERE, LADS!

"BELLE WAS THE *LOVELIEST* GIRL ON THE MISSISSIPPI... A *DELICATE, SHELTERED FLOWER!*"

"AND *SO RICH!*"

PAPA, I THOUGHT WE OUGHT TO PAINT THE MANSION!

NONSENSE! WE'LL JEST BUY US A *NEW* ONE!

AND *NOW* SHE'S COMING TO VISIT! AFTER *ALL* THESE YEARS!

YOU LADS WATCH YOUR MANNERS WHILE SHE'S HERE!

THE TELEGRAM SAYS SHE'S ARRIVING TODAY BY *SHIP!* SHE'S PROBABLY TRAVELING ON HER PRIVATE YACHT! YOU BOYS WAIT HERE!

I'LL RUN TOWN TO THE PIER AND MEET HER!... AND REMEMBER—*BEHAVE!*

GOLLY, I'VE NEVER SEEN UNCA SCROOGE SO EXCITED!

I CAN'T WAIT TO *SEE* THIS— *BELLE* DUCK!

I CAN WAIT! I CAN WAIT *FOREVER!*

SO *DELICATE!* SO *REFINED!* SO *WE'D-BETTER-BEHAVE-WHILE-SHE'S-HERE!* SHE SOUNDS LIKE A REAL PAIN IN THE NECK!

HEY, *KIDS!* CAN YOU TELL ME WHERE I CAN FIND *SCROOGE McDUCK?*

HUH?!

TELL HIM HIS OLD FRIEND *BELLE DUCK* IS LOOKING FOR HIM!

YOU'RE MISS BELLE?

THAT'S RIGHT! HEY, Y'ALL LOOK LIKE GOOD KIDS!...

THE DELICATE... *REFINED* BELLE DUCK?

...HOW WOULD Y'ALL LIKE TO COME FOR A *RIDE* ON MY *RIVERBOAT?*

A RIDE—

ON A *REAL RIVERBOAT?* GOLLY!

LET'S GET OUR HATS!

JUST LIKE IN TOM SAWYER AND HUCK FINN!

MY, WHAT A *DIRTY* OLD COIN!

EXCUSE ME, MA'AM! I'M THE *PAPERBOY!* MR. McDUCK OWES ME FOR DELIVERING THE *GALL STREET JOURNAL!*

I'LL PAY YOU, SONNY! OH, YES... I SHOULD GIVE YOU A LITTLE *TIP*, TOO!

GEE! MR. McDUCK *NEVER* GIVES A TIP!

TAKE *THIS* OLD COIN— WHATEVER IT IS! I'M SURE SCROOGE WILL NEVER MISS IT!

GOSH! THANK YOU, MA'AM!

WE'RE READY TO GO, MISS BELLE!

GOOD! REMIND ME TO TELL SCROOGE THAT I PAID THE PAPERBOY FOR HIM!

WE'LL HAVE A NICE RUN DOWN THE TULEBUG RIVER ON MY BOAT! IT'S CALLED THE *S. S. GILDED LILY!*

GREAT! MAYBE WE'LL FIND UNCA SCROOGE!

HE WENT DOWN TO MEET YOU!

THERE SHE IS, BOYS!

GOLLY! SHE'S *AWESOME!*

I CAN'T UNDERSTAND IT! THE TELEGRAM SAID SHE'D ARRIVE *TODAY!* BUT THERE'S NO *PRIVATE YACHT* HERE... NOTHING BUT THAT BROKEN-DOWN OLD STEAMBOAT!

S. S. GILDED LILY

I'D BETTER READ THE WIRE AGAIN! DID I MAKE SOME GOSHAWFUL *MISTAKE?*

BOYS, I'M BACK! DO YOU REMEMBER WHAT I DID WITH THAT WIRE? BOYS?

THEY'RE GONE! AND... AND... *AWK!*

...*SO* IS MY *1803 HALF-DRUBNIK!* I LEFT IT RIGHT HERE ON THE DESK! I'VE BEEN *ROBBED!*

HALP! IT'S A CATASTROPHE! MY THREE NEPHEWS ARE MISSING! EVEN WORSE... I'M A FORTUNE POORER!

ATTENTION! ≷HRUMPH!≷ THIEVES HAVE STRUCK MR. McDUCK! ALERT THE POLICE... THE AIR PATROL... THE COAST GUARD!

IT'S AN EMERGENCY! FIND THE THREE DUCK NEPHEWS! MORE IMPORTANT... FIND THE ROBBER WHO ROBBED MR. McDUCK!

☐DAILY BUGLE☐

GREAT McDUCK THEFT! REWARD OFFERED

THEY MUST HAVE TAKEN McDUCK FOR BILLIONS!

ANYTIME THAT TIGHTWAD SPENDS MONEY ON A REWARD, YOU CAN BET HE'S WORRIED!

WANTED MAKERS-OFF WITH McDUCK MUNIFICENCE (MAINLY)

I DROPPED THE COIN THAT NICE LADY GAVE ME!... IT WENT DOWN THE DRAIN! OH, WELL—IT WAS AWFULLY RUSTY AND WORN!

GOSH, YOUR RIVERBOAT IS KEEN, MISS BELLE!

I'M GLAD Y'ALL LIKE IT, BOYS! TOO BAD SCROOGE ISN'T ALONG!

YEAH! HE COULD USE A LITTLE FUN!

I DO DECLARE! LOOKS LIKE WE'VE GOT COMPANY!

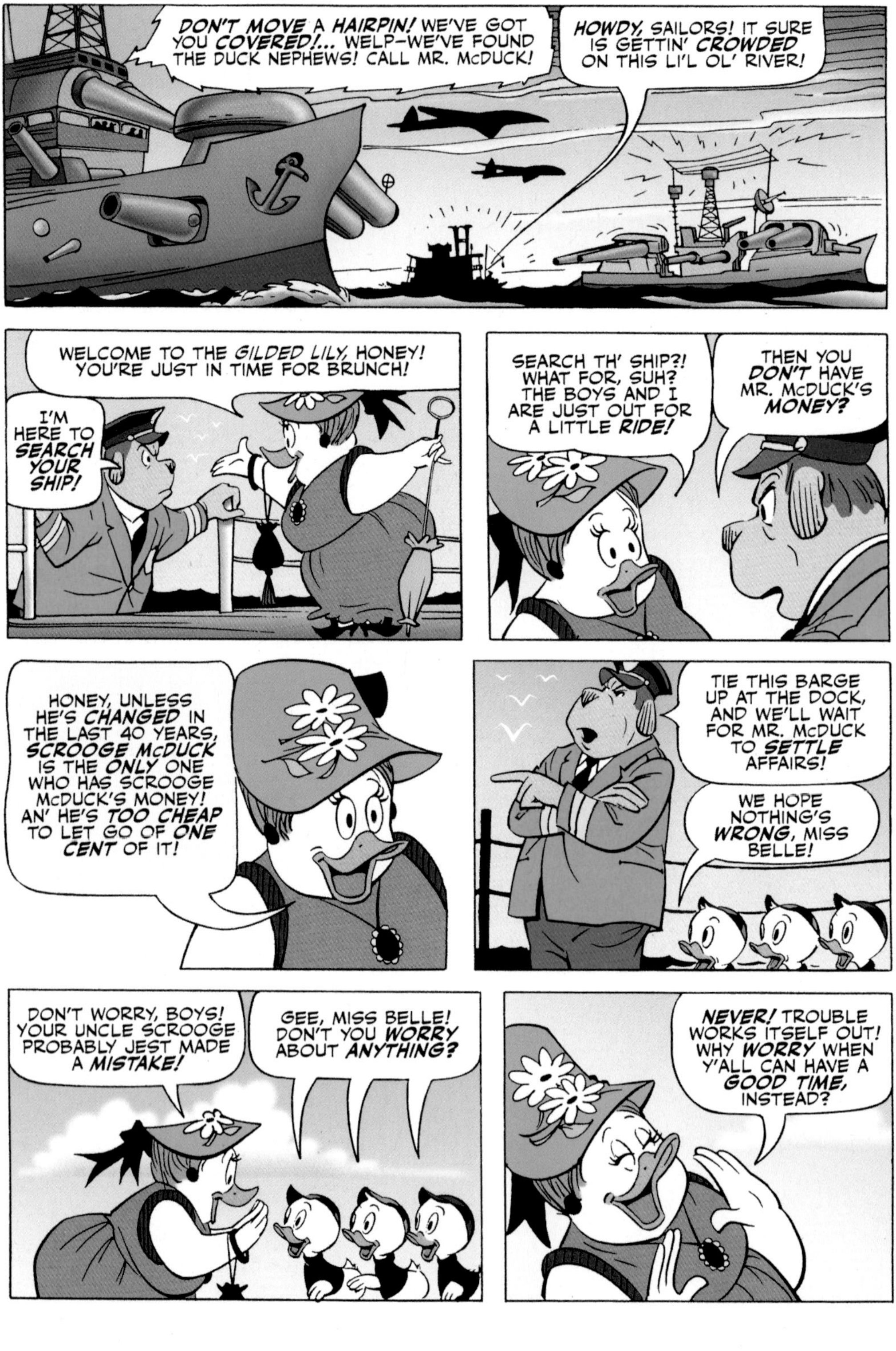
DON'T MOVE A HAIRPIN! WE'VE GOT YOU COVERED!... WELP—WE'VE FOUND THE DUCK NEPHEWS! CALL MR. McDUCK!
HOWDY, SAILORS! IT SURE IS GETTIN' CROWDED ON THIS LI'L OL' RIVER!
WELCOME TO THE GILDED LILY, HONEY! YOU'RE JUST IN TIME FOR BRUNCH!
I'M HERE TO SEARCH YOUR SHIP!
SEARCH TH' SHIP?! WHAT FOR, SUH? THE BOYS AND I ARE JUST OUT FOR A LITTLE RIDE!
THEN YOU DON'T HAVE MR. McDUCK'S MONEY?
HONEY, UNLESS HE'S CHANGED IN THE LAST 40 YEARS, SCROOGE McDUCK IS THE ONLY ONE WHO HAS SCROOGE McDUCK'S MONEY! AN' HE'S TOO CHEAP TO LET GO OF ONE CENT OF IT!
TIE THIS BARGE UP AT THE DOCK, AND WE'LL WAIT FOR MR. McDUCK TO SETTLE AFFAIRS!
WE HOPE NOTHING'S WRONG, MISS BELLE!
DON'T WORRY, BOYS! YOUR UNCLE SCROOGE PROBABLY JEST MADE A MISTAKE!
GEE, MISS BELLE! DON'T YOU WORRY ABOUT ANYTHING?
NEVER! TROUBLE WORKS ITSELF OUT! WHY WORRY WHEN Y'ALL CAN HAVE A GOOD TIME, INSTEAD?

THANK GOODNESS THE LADS ARE SAFE! AND MY HALF-DRUBNIK TOO, I HOPE!

HI, UNCA SCROOGE!

MY *COIN*... THE ONE I LEFT ON THE DESK! WHERE *IS* IT?

GEE! WE DON'T KNOW, UNCA SCROOGE!

THAT DIRTY OL' COIN? WHY, I GAVE IT TO THE NEWS-PAPER BOY FOR A TIP!

YOU *GAVE* IT TO HIM?! HOW *DARE* YOU?!... AND WHO *ARE* YOU?!

UNCA SCROOGE! THIS IS MISS *BELLE DUCK!*

MISS BELLE?! ⌐GULP!⌐ MY, HOW YOU'VE CHANGED.

YOU AIN'T EXACTLY IN DIAPERS YOURSELF, SCROOGE HONEY!

BUT... BUT WHAT ARE YOU DOING ON THIS RUSTY OLD RIVERBOAT?

WELL—SHE AIN'T *FANCY*, BUT SHE'S THE BEST I CAN AFFORD THIS YEAR!

BUT BELLE! WHAT ABOUT ALL YOUR *MONEY?* WHAT ABOUT THE BEAUTIFUL PLANTATION YOU OWNED?

OH, *THAT?* I *SOLD* IT!

YOU DID? YOU MUST HAVE MADE A TIDY PROFIT!

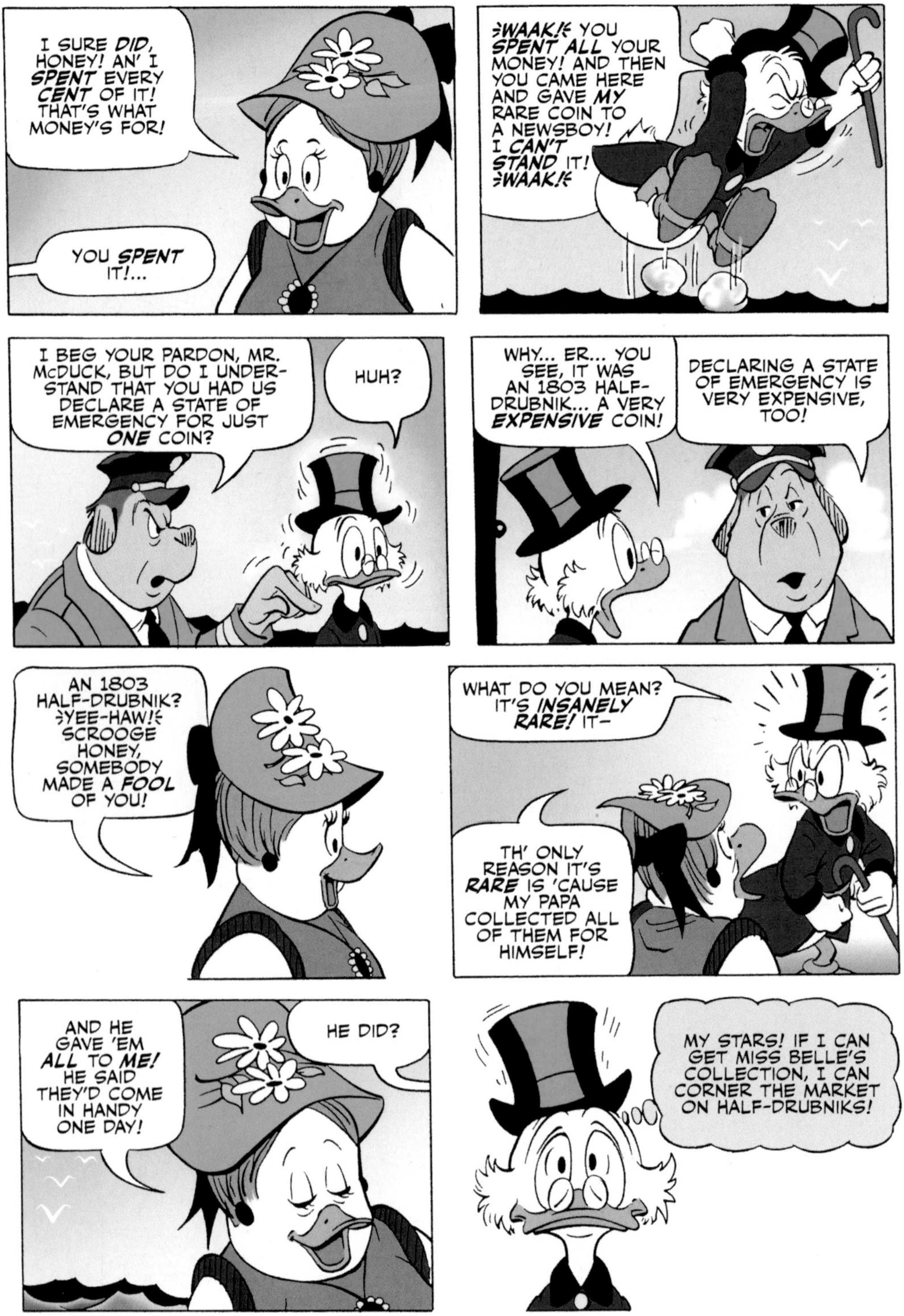

I SURE DID, HONEY! AN' I SPENT EVERY CENT OF IT! THAT'S WHAT MONEY'S FOR!
YOU SPENT IT!...
WAAK! YOU SPENT ALL YOUR MONEY! AND THEN YOU CAME HERE AND GAVE MY RARE COIN TO A NEWSBOY! I CAN'T STAND IT! WAAK!
I BEG YOUR PARDON, MR. McDUCK, BUT DO I UNDERSTAND THAT YOU HAD US DECLARE A STATE OF EMERGENCY FOR JUST ONE COIN?
HUH?
WHY... ER... YOU SEE, IT WAS AN 1803 HALF-DRUBNIK... A VERY EXPENSIVE COIN!
DECLARING A STATE OF EMERGENCY IS VERY EXPENSIVE, TOO!
AN 1803 HALF-DRUBNIK? YEE-HAW! SCROOGE HONEY, SOMEBODY MADE A FOOL OF YOU!
WHAT DO YOU MEAN? IT'S INSANELY RARE! IT—
TH' ONLY REASON IT'S RARE IS 'CAUSE MY PAPA COLLECTED ALL OF THEM FOR HIMSELF!
AND HE GAVE 'EM ALL TO ME! HE SAID THEY'D COME IN HANDY ONE DAY!
HE DID?
MY STARS! IF I CAN GET MISS BELLE'S COLLECTION, I CAN CORNER THE MARKET ON HALF-DRUBNIKS!

UH... I DON'T SUPPOSE YOU'D LET ME HAVE JUST *ONE* HALF-DRUBNIK FOR MY COLLECTION?!

I'LL MAKE A *DEAL* WITH YOU, HONEY...

I SEE EVERYONE'S PRETTY *MAD* 'CAUSE OF THE *FUSS* YOU CAUSED...

WE SURE ARE!

≯GULP!≮

...AN' I WAS THINKING ABOUT THROWING A PARTY, ANYWAY...

WELL?

SO I'LL GIVE YOU MY HALF-DRUBNIK COLLECTION IF YOU'LL PAY FOR THE PARTY!

IT'S A *DEAL!*... WHO'S COMING TO YOUR PARTY, BELLE?

IT'S *YOUR* PARTY, HONEY! AN' THE *WHOLE TOWN* IS COMING!

SCROOGE McDUCK PAYS FOR HOLIDAY!

MISS BELLE SURE KNOWS HOW TO THROW A PARTY!

AND UNCA SCROOGE IS GONNA *KNOW* HOW TO PAY FOR IT!

HERE—HAVE SOME MORE PUNCH, HONEY! IT'S *ALL* ON *SCROOGE!*

THANK YOU, MISS BELLE!

≯SOB! SOB!≮

I SURE LIKE MISS BELLE!

End

UNCLE SCROOGE'S HOME EC 101:

GOING PLACES

Walt Disney

D-2256-04

UNCLE SCROOGE ONLY KEEPS THIS *COUNTRY ESTATE* TO IMPRESS POSH BUSINESS PARTNERS! WONDER WHY HE NEEDS *ME* OUT HERE?

JUST IN TIME, LAD! SCRAPE THE *VARNISH* OFF THE DOOR AND COLLECT IT IN THAT BUCKET!

SNORT! I SEE! YOU WANT *FREE RENOVATING HELP!*

TUT! IF I WERE JUST *RENOVATING*... I WOULDN'T SAVE THE VARNISH! OR THIS *WALLPAPER!* OR—

YOU'RE *NOT* RENOVATING? SO WHAT *ARE* YOU DOING?

MOVING!

!

FWIP

The End

WALT DISNEY'S UNCLE $CROOGE vs.

"the BIGGER OPERATOR"

AND AS *SOON* AS I BROUGHT HIM THE NEWSPAPER, YOUR UNCLE DROPPED TO THE FLOOR AND HAD A RIGHT *TANTRUM!*

J-967

SHOCKED AT THE *PRICE* OF THE PAPER... PERHAPS! OR PERHAPS SOME BAD NEWS IN THE HEADLINES!

GET HIM TO THE COUCH, MEN!

‹HMM!› NOTHING *BAD* HERE—OR EVEN BORING! JUST A NOTICE THAT SOME CHARACTER NAMED *ANTOINE MOUNTEBANK* HAS SET UP SHOP IN DUCKBURG!

WHO...?

PROBABLY A STARTUP COMPANY BOSS...

NO, DARN IT! THE MOST CUNNING CON MAN IN THE WHOLE WIDE WORLD!

WELL! HE HAS RISEN!

⋛SIGH!⋚ YOU'LL RECALL PEOPLE CALL ME THE BIG OPERATOR FOR MY MASTERFUL BUSINESS PLANS!

SO? GET TO THE POINT ABOUT THIS GUY!

⋛SOB! SOB!⋚

MOUNTEBANK CALLS HIMSELF THE BIGGER OPERATOR! HE'S A SUPER ENGINEER WHO CREATES MASTERFUL ROBBERY PLANS, AND...

...AND?

AND HE SELLS THEM!

"BEING A GREAT ARCHITECT, HE CAN ANALYZE ANY BUILDING, VEHICLE, OR ROADWAY... AND MAP OUT ITS WEAK POINTS FOR OTHER CROOKS TO EXPLOIT!"

"THEN, AS A DRAFTSMAN, HE PLOTS OUT THEIR THEFTS—DOWN TO THE MOST MINUTE DETAIL! THAT'S WHY HE'S POPULAR IN THE UNDERWORLD!"

⋛HEH-HEH!⋚

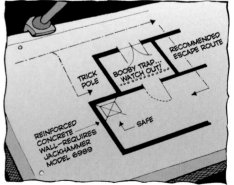

RECOMMENDED ESCAPE ROUTE

TRICK POLE

BOOBY TRAP... WATCH OUT!

SAFE

REINFORCED CONCRETE WALL—REQUIRES JACKHAMMER MODEL 6989

"YOU CAN NEVER PREDICT WHO HIS NEXT CLIENT WILL BE!"

OF *COURSE* IT'S A GOOD PLAN! IT'S *MINE!*

AND MOUNTEBANK *GETS AWAY* WITH IT! HE ALWAYS KEEPS *HIS* HANDS CLEAN!

WHY DON'T THE *POLICE* DO ANYTHING ABOUT HIM?

NO *EVIDENCE* AGAINST HIM, NEPHEW!

HIS *PLANS* LOOK LIKE *FLOOR MODELS* AND *ROADMAPS!* THEY NEVER ACTUALLY *MENTION* THEFT!

BOY, HE *IS* A BIG OPERATOR!

BIGGER OPERATOR! HE PICKED THAT MONIKER JUST TO *MESS* WITH ME... AND IT *WORKED!* ⋛BOO-HOO!⋜

⋛WAK!⋜

SQUISH

MY POOR BILLIONS! SOON TO BE *SCATTERED* FROM THEIR PAPA!

⋛BAWWWWWW!!!⋜

ACT YOUR AGE, UNCLE SCROOGE!

$

WHAT HAPPENED TO BEING *TOUGHER THAN THE TOUGHIES,* AND *SMARTER THAN THE SMARTIES?* OR WAS THAT ALL JUST *TALK?*

≈URK!≈ YOU'RE RIGHT!

I'VE GOT A LOAD OF *GOLD* COMING IN TOMORROW... BUT I'LL PLAY MY *BEST* DEFENSE! NONE OF MOUNTEBANK'S CUSTOMERS WILL GET THEIR HANDS ON *THIS!*

WELL SAID!

COMES THE DAWN!

BOY, OLD McDUCK THOUGHT UP A *PLUM* OF A THIEF-FOILING PLAN! HE'S GOT *NOTHING* TO WORRY ABOUT!

YOU SAID IT!

ROARR

VROOM VROOM

MCD AQUA-SUPPLIES

ARMORED TRUCK WITH A PHONY NAME— *CHECK!* GET OUT 12 HOURS AHEAD OF SCHEDULE...

CHECK!

AND TO KEEP TRACK OF ANY GOONS TRYING FUNNY BUSINESS... WE EVEN GOT A *PERISCOPE!*

≈HEH!≈ LIKE A *SUBMARINE* ON WHEELS!

ROARR

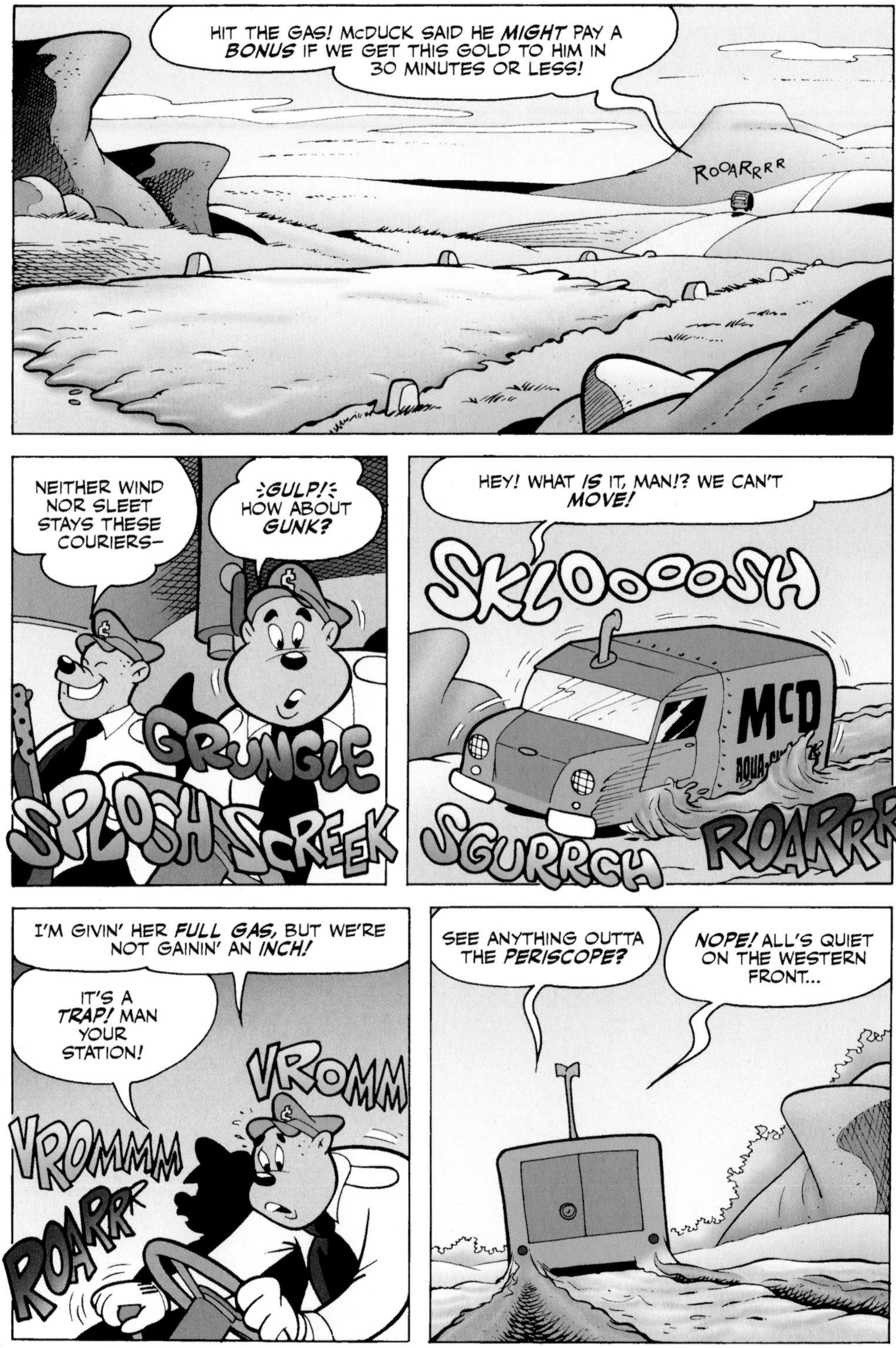
HIT THE GAS! McDUCK SAID HE MIGHT PAY A BONUS IF WE GET THIS GOLD TO HIM IN 30 MINUTES OR LESS!
ROOARRRR
NEITHER WIND NOR SLEET STAYS THESE COURIERS—
GULP! HOW ABOUT GUNK?
GRUNGLE
SPLOSH
SCREEK
HEY! WHAT IS IT, MAN!? WE CAN'T MOVE!
SKLOOOOSH
McD
SGURRCH
ROARRR
I'M GIVIN' HER FULL GAS, BUT WE'RE NOT GAININ' AN INCH!
IT'S A TRAP! MAN YOUR STATION!
VROMM
VROMMM
ROARRR
SEE ANYTHING OUTTA THE PERISCOPE?
NOPE! ALL'S QUIET ON THE WESTERN FRONT...

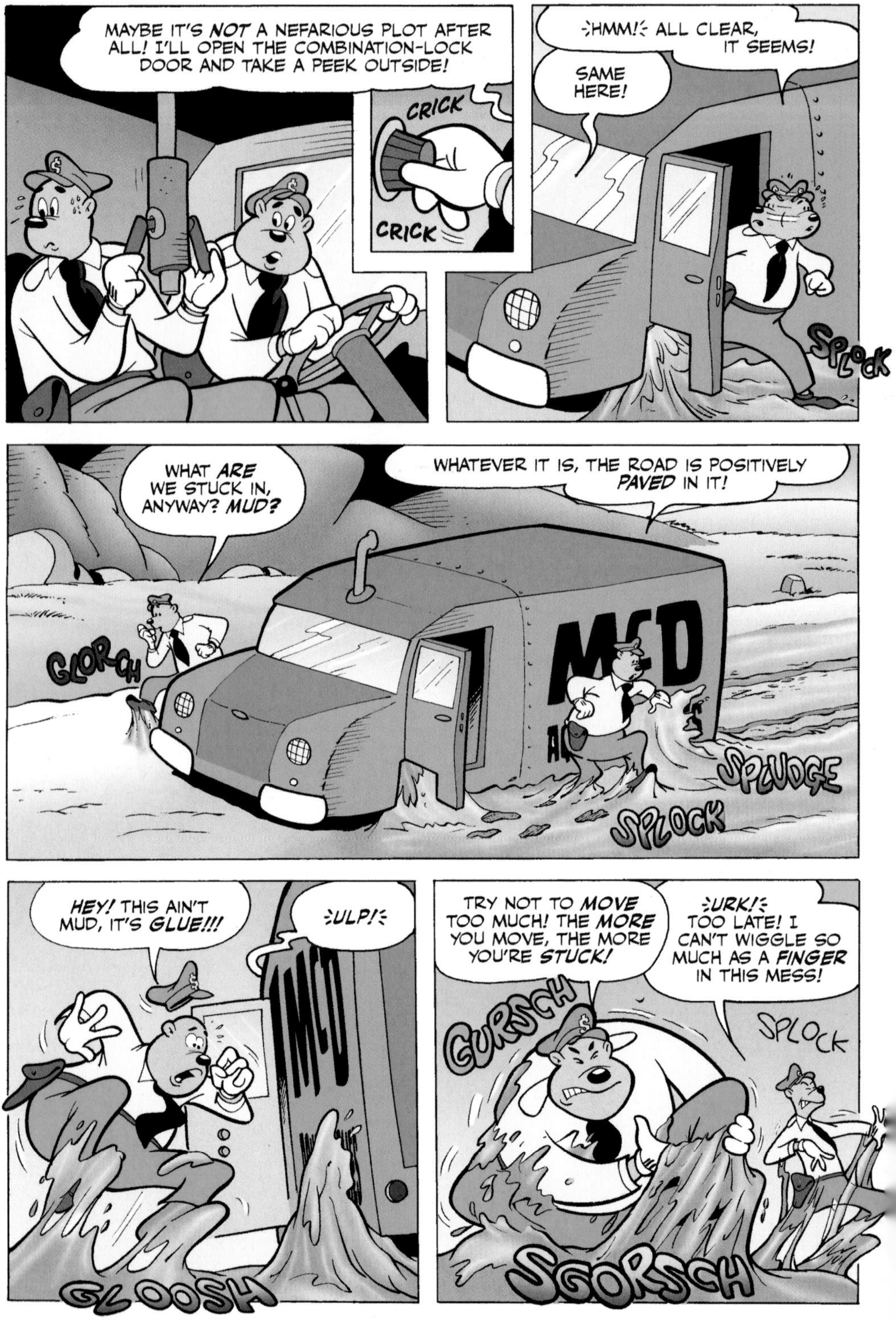
MAYBE IT'S NOT A NEFARIOUS PLOT AFTER ALL! I'LL OPEN THE COMBINATION-LOCK DOOR AND TAKE A PEEK OUTSIDE!
CRICK
CRICK
HMM! ALL CLEAR, IT SEEMS!
SAME HERE!
SPLOCK
WHAT ARE WE STUCK IN, ANYWAY? MUD?
WHATEVER IT IS, THE ROAD IS POSITIVELY PAVED IN IT!
GLORCH
MCD
SPLUDGE
SPLOCK
HEY! THIS AIN'T MUD, IT'S GLUE!!!
ULP!
GLOOSH
TRY NOT TO MOVE TOO MUCH! THE MORE YOU MOVE, THE MORE YOU'RE STUCK!
URK! TOO LATE! I CAN'T WIGGLE SO MUCH AS A FINGER IN THIS MESS!
GURSCH
SPLOCK
SGORSCH

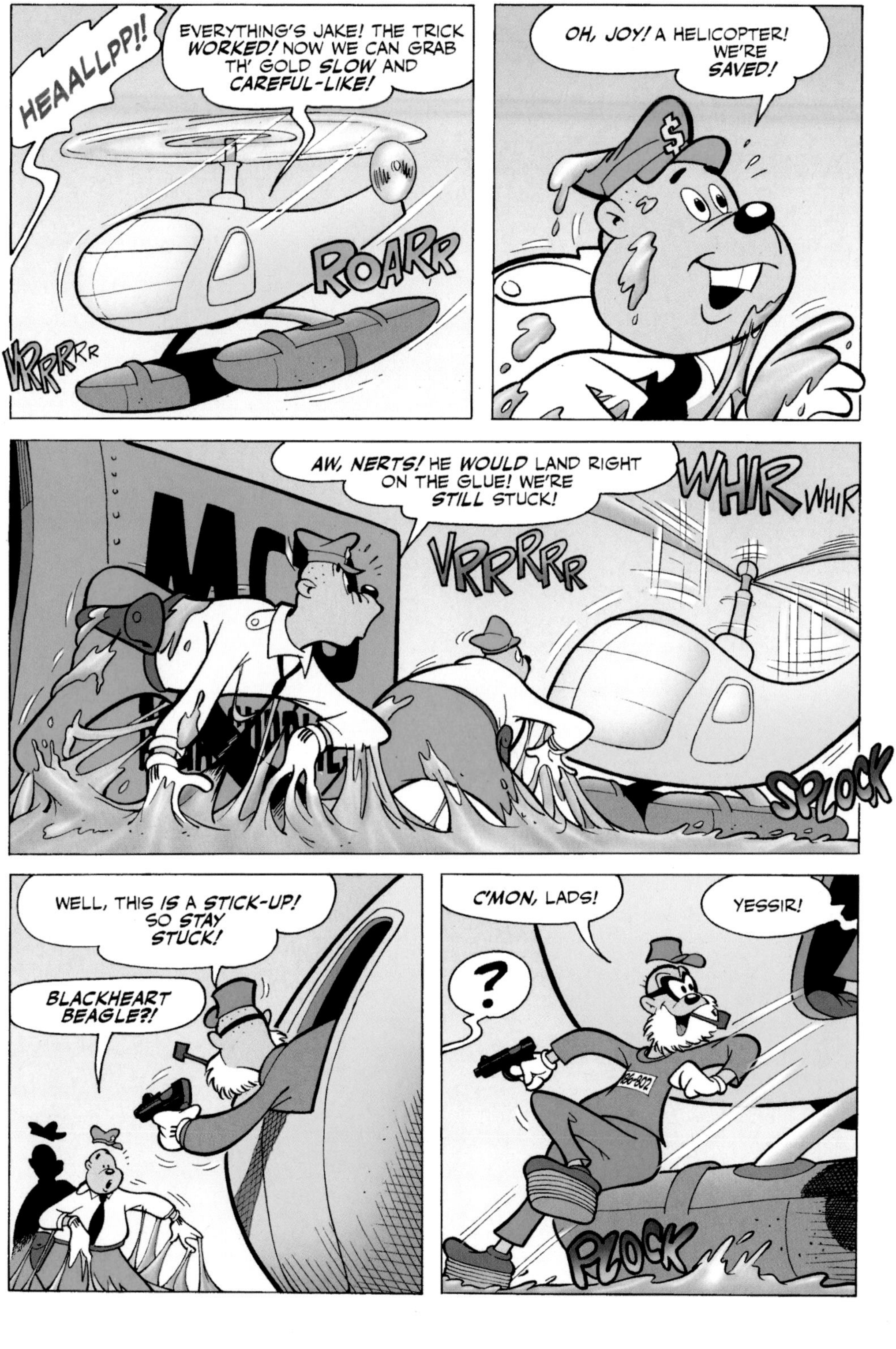
HEAALLPP!!
EVERYTHING'S JAKE! THE TRICK WORKED! NOW WE CAN GRAB TH' GOLD SLOW AND CAREFUL-LIKE!
ROARR
VRRRRRR
OH, JOY! A HELICOPTER! WE'RE SAVED!
AW, NERTS! HE WOULD LAND RIGHT ON THE GLUE! WE'RE STILL STUCK!
WHIR WHIR
VRRRRR
SPLOCK
WELL, THIS IS A STICK-UP! SO STAY STUCK!
BLACKHEART BEAGLE?!
C'MON, LADS!
YESSIR!
?
PLOCK

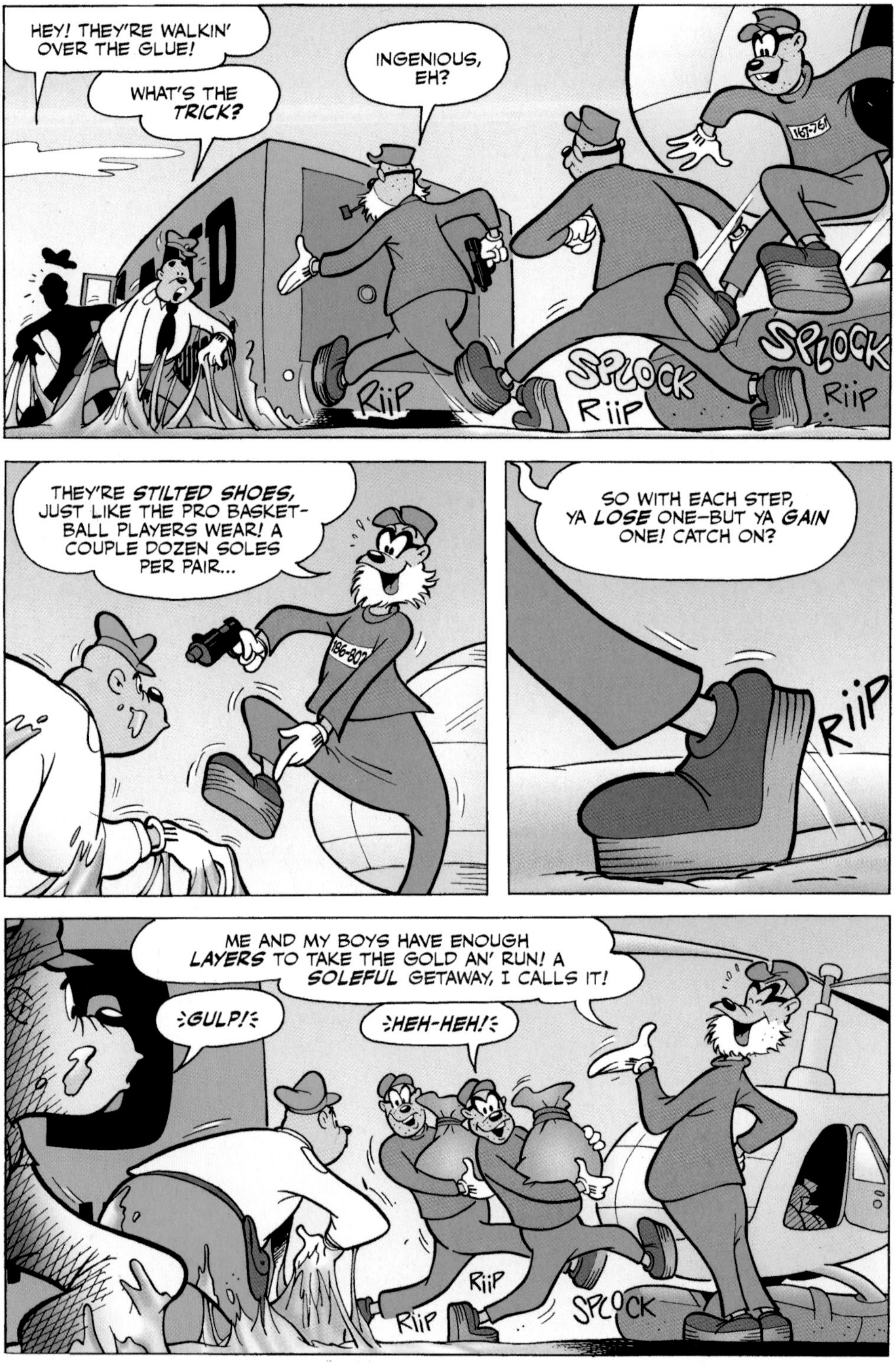
HEY! THEY'RE WALKIN' OVER THE GLUE!
WHAT'S THE TRICK?
INGENIOUS, EH?
SPLOCK
RIIP
SPLOCK
RIIP
RIIP
THEY'RE STILTED SHOES, JUST LIKE THE PRO BASKET-BALL PLAYERS WEAR! A COUPLE DOZEN SOLES PER PAIR...
SO WITH EACH STEP, YA LOSE ONE—BUT YA GAIN ONE! CATCH ON?
RIIP
ME AND MY BOYS HAVE ENOUGH LAYERS TO TAKE THE GOLD AN' RUN! A SOLEFUL GETAWAY, I CALLS IT!
GULP!
HEH-HEH!
RIIP
RIIP
SPLOCK

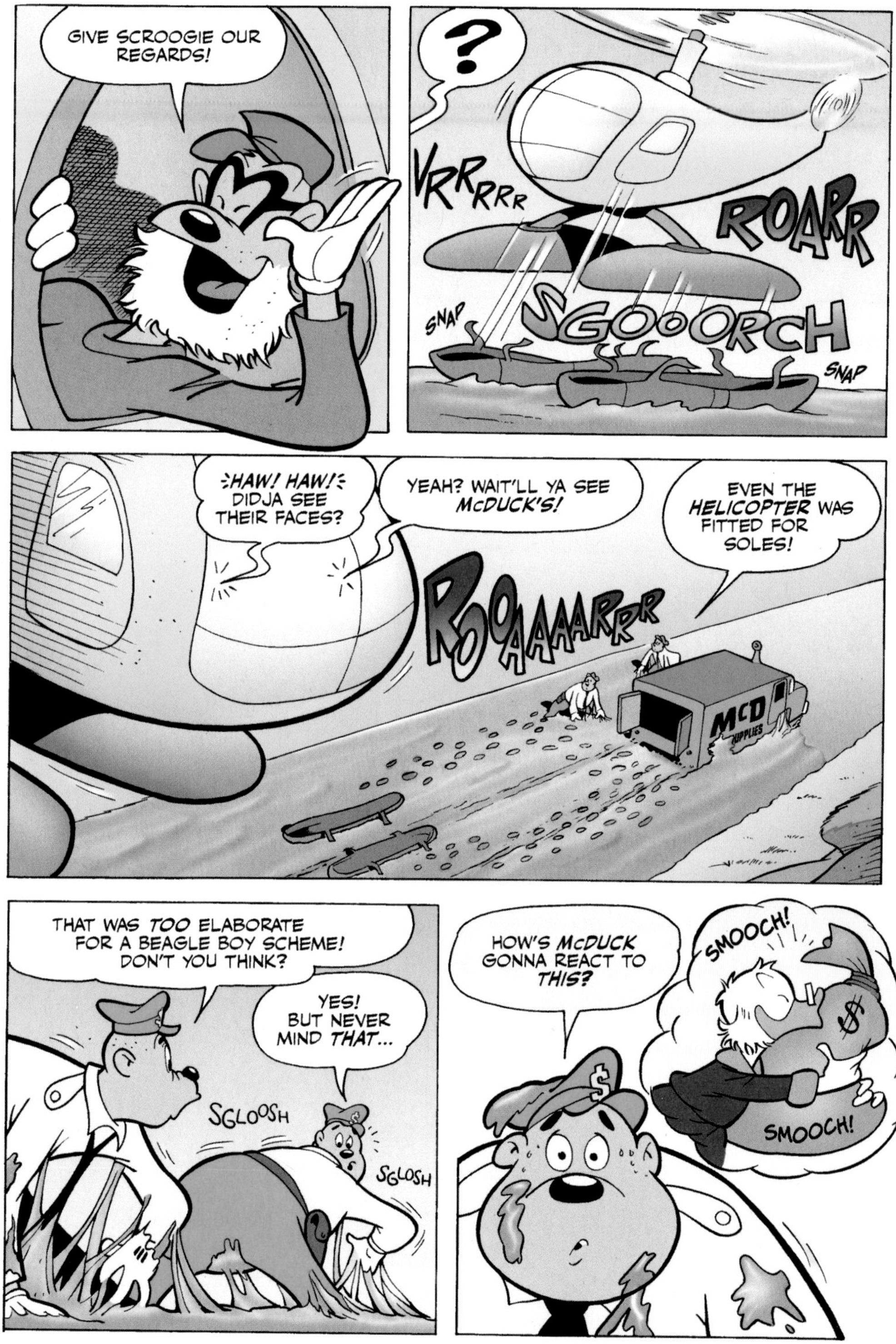
GIVE SCROOGIE OUR REGARDS!
?
VRRRRRR
ROARR
SNAP
SGOOoORCH
SNAP
HAW! HAW! DIDJA SEE THEIR FACES?
YEAH? WAIT'LL YA SEE McDUCK'S!
EVEN THE HELICOPTER WAS FITTED FOR SOLES!
ROOAAAARRR
McD
THAT WAS TOO ELABORATE FOR A BEAGLE BOY SCHEME! DON'T YOU THINK?
YES! BUT NEVER MIND THAT...
SGLOOSH
SGLOSH
HOW'S McDUCK GONNA REACT TO THIS?
SMOOCH!
SMOOCH!

YEAH... *HOW?*

POOR UNCA SCROOGE!

C'MON, GUYS—USE YOUR HEADS! YOU TELL HIM ABOUT A *SUPER-HEIST* LIKE IT'S THE WEATHER?

GEEZ, MR. DUCK...

HOW'S HE DOING?

HE'LL MAKE IT!

⸚GURF!⸚

FSSSSₛₛ

$a CO₃
400 LBS.

GYRO GEARLOOSE'S *COMPRESSED DOLLAR-HYDROGEN MIX* IS THE ONLY THING THAT CAN REVIVE UNCA SCROOGE FROM DEVASTATION!

⸚BELCH!⸚

$a CO₃
400 LBS.

LATER...

NO DOUBT ABOUT IT, BOYS! *MOUNTEBANK* PLANNED THIS BEAGLE BOY RAID!

WE NEED TO TEACH THAT BAD GENIUS A *LESSON* BEFORE HE WREAKS ANY MORE HAVOC!

WHAT'S THE PLAN?

HM! *LAST* DEFENSE DIDN'T WORK! WE NEED TO GET AT HIM A *DIFFERENT* WAY!

A *MODERN* WAY! A *SLICK* WAY!

BUT WHAT WAY?

ESPIONAGE! THAT'S THE TICKET! SEND A *SECRET AGENT* INTO MOUNTEBANK'S *HOME* TO GET THE GOODS ON HIM!

ULP!

WE'LL CRACK *EVERY* LAST PLAN THAT DEVIL IS PREPARING...

THUMP

...AND THEN WE'LL *MOVE ON* TO MR. MOUNTEBANK'S *PATRONS!*

I NEED A *DECISIVE* SPY! *COURAGEOUS! ABLE-BODIED!* AND ABOVE ALL—HE MUST WORK ON A *VOLUNTEER* BASIS!

:HEH!: SO *WHO* MIGHT THIS HARDY *UNPAID INTERN* BE?

COME, DONALD, THIS IS NO TIME FOR JOKES! YOU DON'T WANT YOUR *BOSS* TO GO *BROKE*, DO YOU?

WELL, WHEN YOU PUT IT *THAT* WAY...

AT POLICE HEADQUARTERS!

EXCELLENT! A PERFECT COVER!

FRONT

PROFILE

FINGERPRINTS →

AND SINCE YOU WON'T BE RISKING... ER, *USING* ANY OF *OUR* MEN, WE'LL BE *HAPPY* TO GIVE YOUR NEPHEW SOME *FREE* HELP!

:HEH!:

:GRUNT!:

SADLY, WE CAN'T ARREST MOUNTEBANK FOR *DRAWING UP* HYPOTHETICAL THEFT PLANS, *OR* SELLING THEM...

NO, A PITY!

...BUT WE CAN STILL *FIND OUT* WHAT THE PLANS ARE, AND *SABOTAGE THEM!*

EXACTLY!

THUK

THAT'S ALL WELL AND GOOD! BUT HOW DO I *INVADE* MOUNTEBANK'S DIGS?

WE GOT A TIP-OFF THAT MOUNTEBANK IS LOOKING TO HIRE A *HEAD BUTLER*...

AND NOT JUST ANYONE WILL DO! IT HAS TO BE SOMEONE HE CAN *TRUST!*

SO WHAT?

SO *YOU* APPLY WITH THIS *NEW* IDENTITY AND *FALSE CRIMINAL RECORD* WE COOKED UP FOR YOU!

WHAT— MY *OWN* ISN'T ENOUGH?

AT THE MOUNTEBANK ESTATE!

WELL, HERE GOES!

ANTOINE MOUNTEBANK
ENGINEERING SPECIALIST

RiiiiiNGGG

WHO GOES THERE?

GREETINGS!

AWRIGHT, CHUM! YA WANTED A BUTLER... SO HERE I AM!

HEY, HOW DID YOU KNOW I NEEDED A BUTLER!?

NEWS TRAVELS FAST! SO HOW'S ABOUT IT?

WELL...

CHOMP
CHOMP

HOW DO I KNOW YOU'RE... ¿AHEM!¿ TRUSTWORTHY? WHAT ARE YOUR QUALIFICATIONS FOR THIS POSITION?

MEH! READ THIS, PALLY!

CHOMP CHOMP

WHIT

¿HMM!¿ QUACKIE DE FISHTAIL! PETTY THIEF AND EXTORTIONIST BY TRADE! WELL, YOU *MIGHT* DO...

CHOMP! CHOMP

...BUT WHAT KIND OF NAME IS *DE FISHTAIL??*

OH, SIMPLE!

CHOMP CHOMP

ME WHOLE FAMILY'S EITHER AS *QUIET* AS FISHES... OR *SLEEPIN'* WITH 'EM!

SO! USED TO THE CRIMINAL ELEMENT, EH? YOU'RE HIRED! FOLLOW ME!

FOR *WHAT?*

YOUR FIRST *BUTLERLY DUTY,* JEEVES!

¿WAK!¿

AND SO...

:GRR!: SECRET AGENT, EH!? ESPIONAGE! @!$*%! MISERABLE MISER...

MUCH LATER...

:PANT!: FINISHED! :PUFF!: YOUR DISHES IS GRIME-FREE, BOSS!

EXCELLENT! NOW THAT YOU'RE FINALLY DONE...

...YOU CAN MOW THE LAWN... VACUUM THE RUGS... SCRUB THE FLOORS... BLAH BLAH BLAH BLAH!

SIGH!

THAT EVENING!

HERE'S DINNER! COOKED TO POIFECTION!

FINE! FINE!

SAY, BOSS! SPEAKIN' ONE NO-GOOD TO ANOTHER... WHY'S THAT DOOR OVER THERE ALWAYS LOCKED?

SLURP!

THAT'S MY *PRIVATE STUDIO!* IT'S OFF LIMITS TO EVERYONE... INCLUDING *YOU!* SAVVY?

GOT IT!

YOU'RE TO LOOK AFTER THE *HOUSE*—BUT *NOTHING* BEYOND THAT DOOR! SLURP!

YESSIR! YESSIR!

≑HAR!≑ WHAT A *SAP!* HE'S PLAYED RIGHT INTO MY HANDS! AND AS SOON AS HE'S ASLEEP...

"...THE *BUTLER* WORKS *OVERTIME!*"

SNOOZING LIKE A LOG! NOW TO BUSINESS!

≑HEH-HEH!≑ DOES THAT GUY REALLY THINK HE CAN OUTWIT A *TRAINED SECRET AGENT* WITH A McDUCK *SKELETON KEY?*

THE POLICE TAUGHT ME A WHOLE MESS OF TRICKS! THIS CASE WILL SOON BE *CRACKED!*

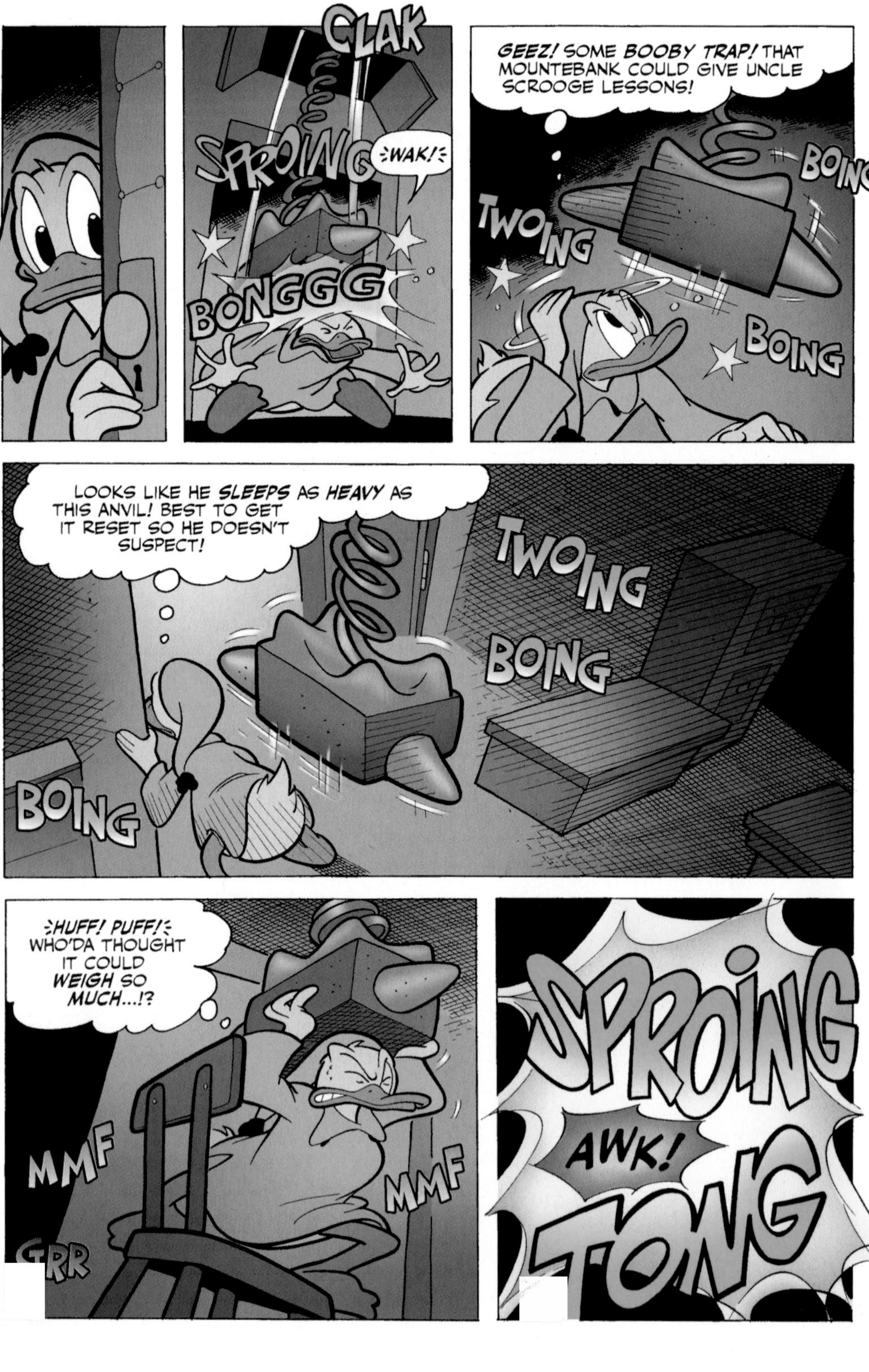
CLAK
SPROING
WAK!
BONGGG
GEEZ! SOME BOOBY TRAP! THAT MOUNTEBANK COULD GIVE UNCLE SCROOGE LESSONS!
BOING
TWOING
BOING
LOOKS LIKE HE SLEEPS AS HEAVY AS THIS ANVIL! BEST TO GET IT RESET SO HE DOESN'T SUSPECT!
TWOING
BOING
BOING
HUFF! PUFF! WHO'DA THOUGHT IT COULD WEIGH SO MUCH...!?
MMF
MMF
GRR
SPROING
AWK!
TONG

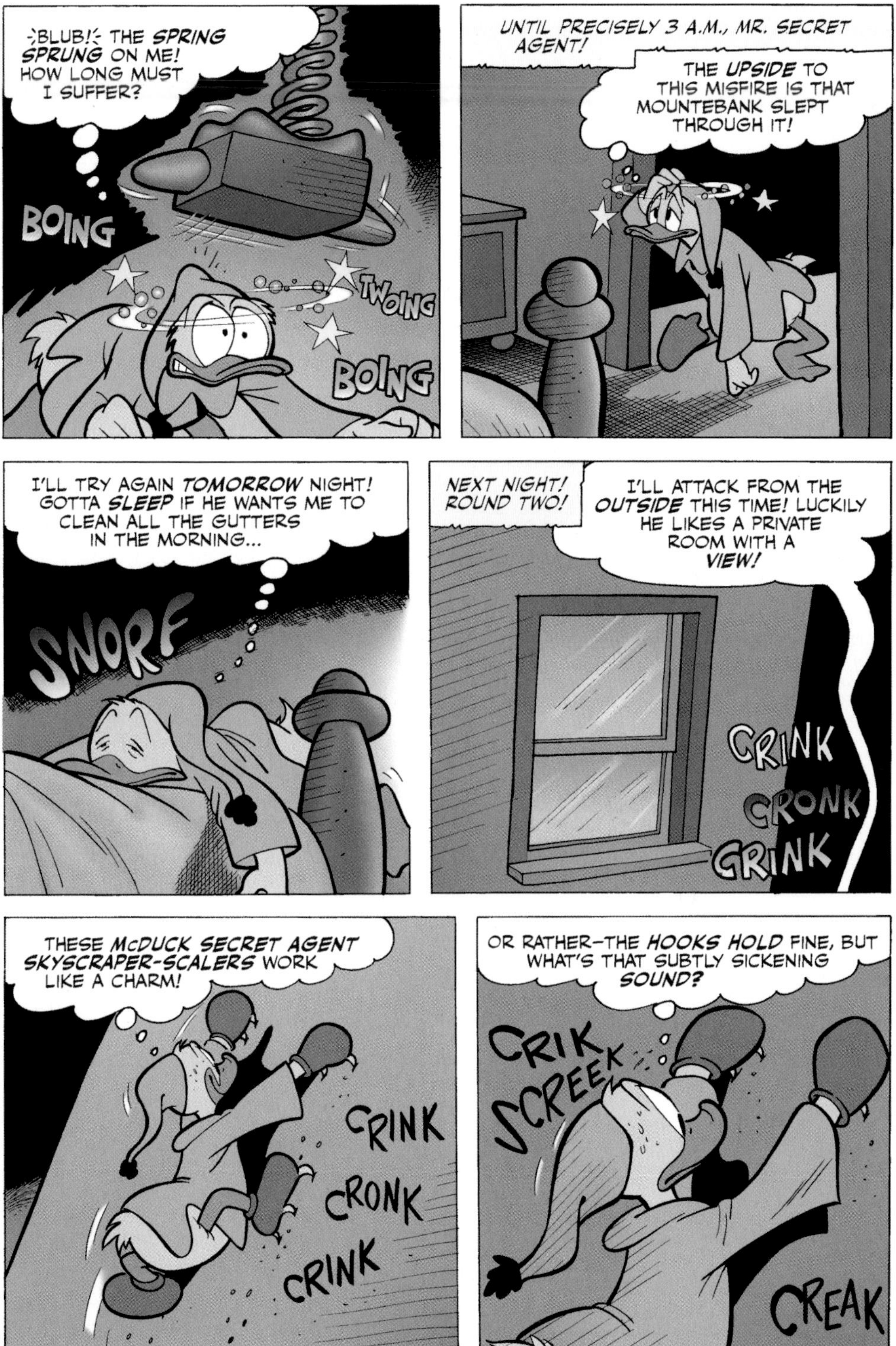

BLUB! THE SPRING SPRUNG ON ME! HOW LONG MUST I SUFFER?
BOING
TWOING
BOING
UNTIL PRECISELY 3 A.M., MR. SECRET AGENT!
THE UPSIDE TO THIS MISFIRE IS THAT MOUNTEBANK SLEPT THROUGH IT!
I'LL TRY AGAIN TOMORROW NIGHT! GOTTA SLEEP IF HE WANTS ME TO CLEAN ALL THE GUTTERS IN THE MORNING...
SNORF
NEXT NIGHT! ROUND TWO!
I'LL ATTACK FROM THE OUTSIDE THIS TIME! LUCKILY HE LIKES A PRIVATE ROOM WITH A VIEW!
CRINK
CRONK
GRINK
THESE McDUCK SECRET AGENT SKYSCRAPER-SCALERS WORK LIKE A CHARM!
CRINK
CRONK
CRINK
OR RATHER—THE HOOKS HOLD FINE, BUT WHAT'S THAT SUBTLY SICKENING SOUND?
CRIK
SCREEK
CREAK

AUGGGGH!!!

SCRONK

CRASH

PREDICTABLY!

YOU AND YOUR *MALFUNCTIONING MANUFACTURING!* AND WHAT'S MORE, I HAD TO CONVINCE MOUNTEBANK I GOT THIS FROM A SLIP IN THE *BATHTUB!*

≤TSK! TSK!≥

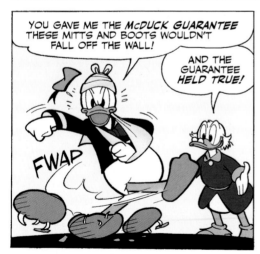

YOU GAVE ME THE *McDUCK GUARANTEE* THESE MITTS AND BOOTS WOULDN'T FALL OFF THE WALL!

AND THE GUARANTEE *HELD TRUE!*

FWAP

YOU FAILED BECAUSE THE *WALL* FELL OFF THE *BUILDING!*

≤GRUNT!≥

BAH! THIS WHOLE *ESPIONAGE* ACT IS A BUST! SPY STUFF WON'T GET US INTO MOUNTEBANK'S STUDIO! WE NEED A *NEW STRATEGY...*

...AND *QUICK!* BEFORE LEAVING, I HEARD HIM TAKE A BUNCH OF *NEW* ORDERS FOR CRIME PLANS!

YEAH! ⸲GRUMBLE! GRUMBLE!⸲

WHAT TO DO? WHAT TO DO?

C'MON! ANY *TRICKS* UP YOUR MOTH-EATEN SLEEVES?

NONE AT THE MOMENT, NEPHEW! BEST YOU GET BACK TO MOUNTEBANK'S HOUSE!

YOU'RE SENDING ME BACK WITH *NOTHING!?*

DON'T WORRY! IF I *THINK* OF A PLAN... YOU'LL BE THE *FIRST* TO KNOW, DONALD!

DAYS LATER!

IT'S A SHAME THIS GUY'S A CRIMINAL MASTERMIND! HE *PAYS* BETTER THAN UNCLE SCROOGE!

RiiiNNGG

BRUSH

BRUSH

THERE'S THE DOORBELL! ANSWER IT!

YESSIR!

MMM'YESSSS?

ER... *YO!* I'M SLIM PICKIN AND—
≷GULP!≶

YOU WISH TO SEE *MAHSTAH?*

UM... NO... YA DON'T—

WHAT'S GOING ON? WHO'S THERE?

THIS *GENTLEMAN* WISHES TO SEE YOU... I THINK!

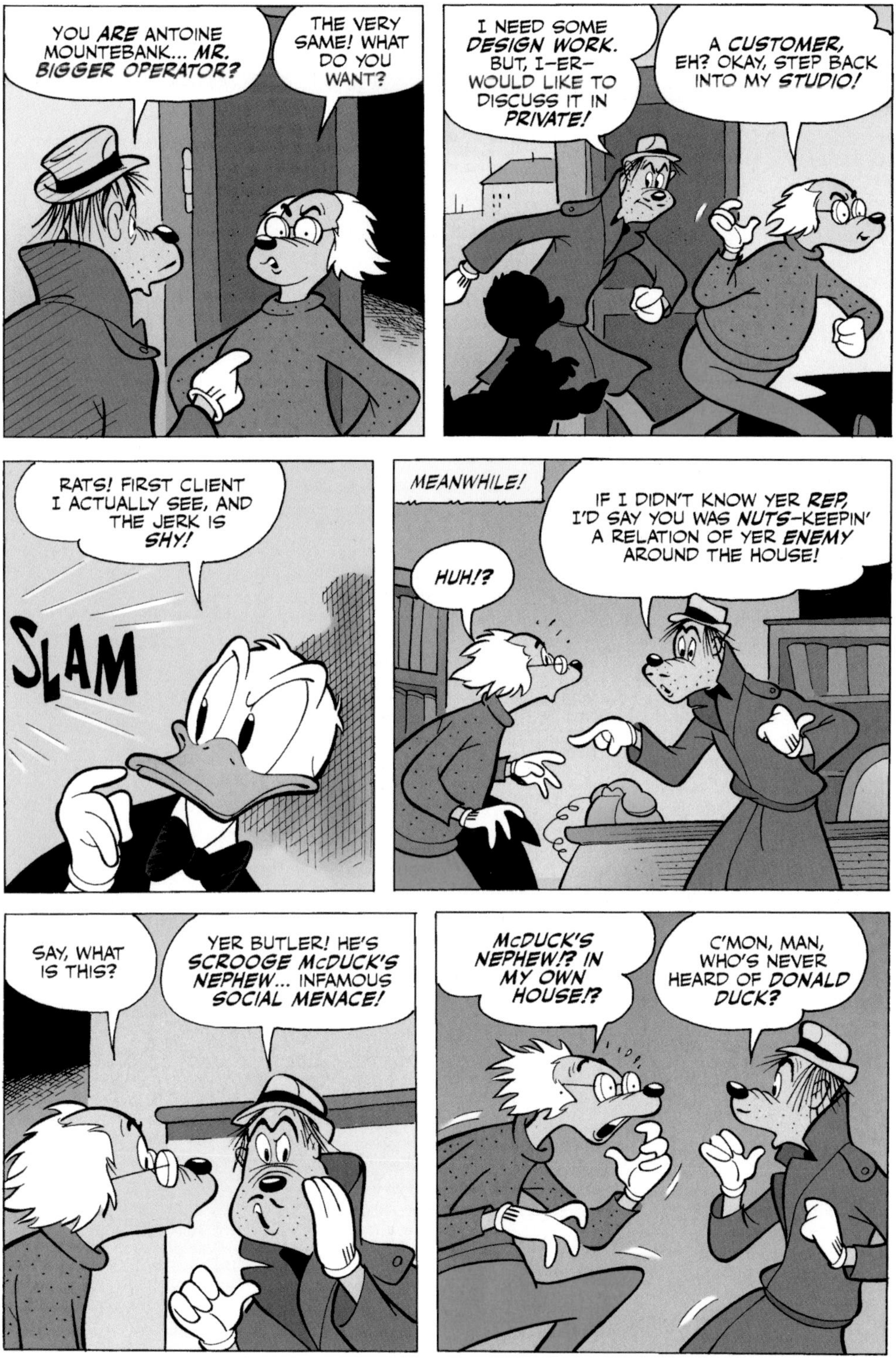
YOU ARE ANTOINE MOUNTEBANK... MR. BIGGER OPERATOR?
THE VERY SAME! WHAT DO YOU WANT?
I NEED SOME DESIGN WORK. BUT, I–ER– WOULD LIKE TO DISCUSS IT IN PRIVATE!
A CUSTOMER, EH? OKAY, STEP BACK INTO MY STUDIO!
RATS! FIRST CLIENT I ACTUALLY SEE, AND THE JERK IS SHY!
SLAM
MEANWHILE!
IF I DIDN'T KNOW YER REP, I'D SAY YOU WAS NUTS–KEEPIN' A RELATION OF YER ENEMY AROUND THE HOUSE!
HUH!?
SAY, WHAT IS THIS?
YER BUTLER! HE'S SCROOGE McDUCK'S NEPHEW... INFAMOUS SOCIAL MENACE!
McDUCK'S NEPHEW!? IN MY OWN HOUSE!?
C'MON, MAN, WHO'S NEVER HEARD OF DONALD DUCK?

I ONLY KNOW *RICH CROOKS,* BUDDY!

HE MUST BE A SPY! WHATCHA GONNA DO?

NOTHING... *YET!* I'VE GOT PLANS FOR— I MEAN, HE COULD *NEVER* OUTTHINK *ME!* LET'S TALK *BUSINESS...*

AN HOUR LATER!

PHOOEY! I CAN'T HEAR A THING! THEY'RE CHIT-CHATTING AS QUIET AS...

÷WAK!÷

WHISH

SPLAT

S'LONG, ANTOINE! AND *THANKS* FOR THE—UM— BANK DESIGNS!

÷HEH! HEH!÷ GOOD LUCK!

HEY, LAZYBONES! SEE MY GUEST TO THE DOOR!

OKAY, BOSS!

THAT LITTLE SQUIRT WILL PLAY RIGHT INTO MY HANDS! SO MUCH FOR McDUCK'S *BIG OPERATIONS!*

GOOD-BYE, MISTER!

CIAO, CHUM!

Panel 1:

THAT NIGHT!

ROUGH EVENING, SIR?

ICK! WHAT A HEADACHE! I'M TURNING IN!

Panel 2:

EVEN A *GENIUS* CAN HAVE AN *OFF DAY!* ICK!

ULP! HE LEFT HIS STUDIO DOOR *OPEN!*

Panel 3:

I'M TAKING A SLEEPING PILL! NOT THAT I NEED IT—I COULD SLEEP THROUGH *ANYTHING!*

'NIGHT, BOSS! PLEASANT DREAMS!

U-DOZE

Panel 4:

SUCCESS?

⸓HEH!⸓ WHAT A BREAK! NOW I CAN FINALLY SABOTAGE HIS PLANS IN *PEACE!*

TOING

TOING

Panel 5:

NOPE!

WHAT A *MESS!* HOW AM I SUPPOSED TO FIND—*EH?*

⸓TEE-HEE!⸓ HE'S TAKING THE BAIT!

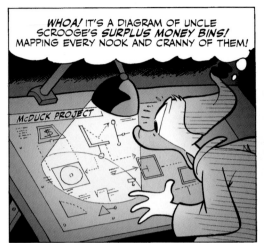

WHOA! IT'S A DIAGRAM OF UNCLE SCROOGE'S SURPLUS MONEY BINS! MAPPING EVERY NOOK AND CRANNY OF THEM!

I'LL USE MY SPY PHONE TO SNAP SOME HIGH-RES PHOTOS OF THE PLAN!

CLIK

CLIK

CLIK

NOW TO TIP OFF UNCLE SCROOGE!

FELL FOR IT HOOK AND LINE, YOU STINKER!

SOON...

EGAD! SO MOUNTEBANK'S PLANNING TO RAID MY SURPLUS BINS, HUH?

WE'VE GOT THE DROP ON THAT WEASEL NOW! GREAT WORK, DONALD!

HEAR, HEAR!

BONK

YOU GO BACK TO YOUR REGULAR DUTIES, NEPHEW! I'LL HANDLE THINGS FROM HERE!

TOO BAD! YOU HAVEN'T SEEN THE FULL EXTENT OF MY SPY CAPABILITIES YET!

PAT PAT

AND SO...

SCROOGE HAS HIS SURPLUS BINS SET UP LIKE A *FORTRESS!* BUT IT WILL AVAIL HIM NAUGHT!

HE'S SO WRAPPED UP IN *THEM* THAT THE DEFENSES AROUND HIS *MAIN* BIN ARE AT AN ALL-TIME *LOW!*

WAIT TILL THE *BIG* OPERATOR SEES WHAT THE *BIGGER* OPERATOR HAS IN STORE!

ROARRR

LET THOSE PETTY THIEVES AND BEAGLE BOYS HAVE THEIR *CHEAP THRILLS!* I'VE WAITED MY WHOLE LIFE FOR *THIS* HEIST... THE *BIG* ONE!

GENIUS *AND* RICHES! WHAT MORE COULD I ASK FOR? ⸝HA-HA-HA!⸜

VROOOOMM

THE *GREAT ROBBERY* IS ON!

MOVE OUT—AND BE *QUIET!* THE ELEMENT OF SURPRISE IS ESSENTIAL!

WE'RE READY WHEN YOU ARE, SIR!

SHEESH! WHO KNEW A TANK WAS SO LOUD?

THEY'RE GONE! NOW TO BUSINESS!

ROARRRr

THIS WASTE TRUCK WAS ALONE AND UNPROTECTED! SO I *STOLE* IT! NO ONE WILL EVER KNOW!

VROOM

VROOM

DUCKBURG WASTE REMOVAL

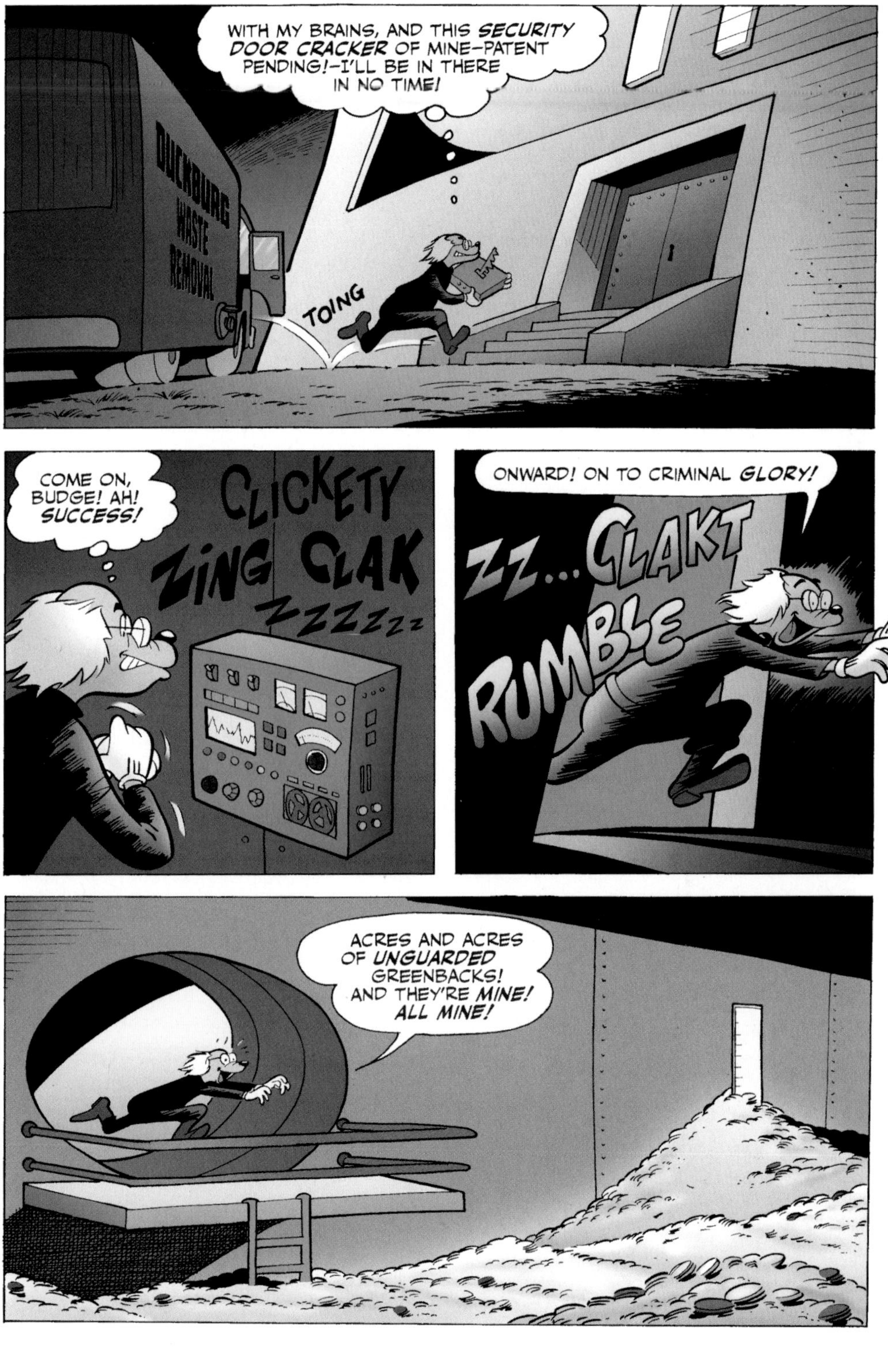
WITH MY BRAINS, AND THIS SECURITY DOOR CRACKER OF MINE—PATENT PENDING!—I'LL BE IN THERE IN NO TIME!
DUCKBURG WASTE REMOVAL
TOING
COME ON, BUDGE! AH! SUCCESS!
CLICKETY
ZING CLAK
ZZZZzz
ONWARD! ON TO CRIMINAL GLORY!
ZZ... CLAKT
RUMBLE
ACRES AND ACRES OF UNGUARDED GREENBACKS! AND THEY'RE MINE! ALL MINE!

UM, *REALLY!?*

:*ULP!*: WHO'S *THERE!?*

SLIM PICKIN!? YOU?

NATCH! I KNEW YER *EGO* WOULD GETCHA WHEN I TOLD YA ABOUT SCROOGE'S TRICK! I KNEW YOU'D TRY TA PULL *SOMETHIN'...*

...SO I FOLLOWED! I DO TRUST YA *ARE* A GENIUS AND *WILL* TALK BUSINESS!

A-HEH! CERTAINLY!

THERE'S *PLENTY* FOR US TO SHARE! YOU KNOW, HONOR AMONG THIEVES AN' ALL THAT!

THIEVES, EH?

OF COURSE I'M A *THIEF!* THAT'S WHY I'M HERE, THAT'S WHY YOU'RE... HEY, WHY *ARE* YOU HERE, ANYWAY?

TO GET THE DROP ON *YOU, SIR!*

YOU OVERREACHED THIS TIME, *MR. MOUNTEBANK!* AND YOU JUST *CONFESSED EVERYTHING* TO DUCKBURG'S FINEST!

:*GASP!*:

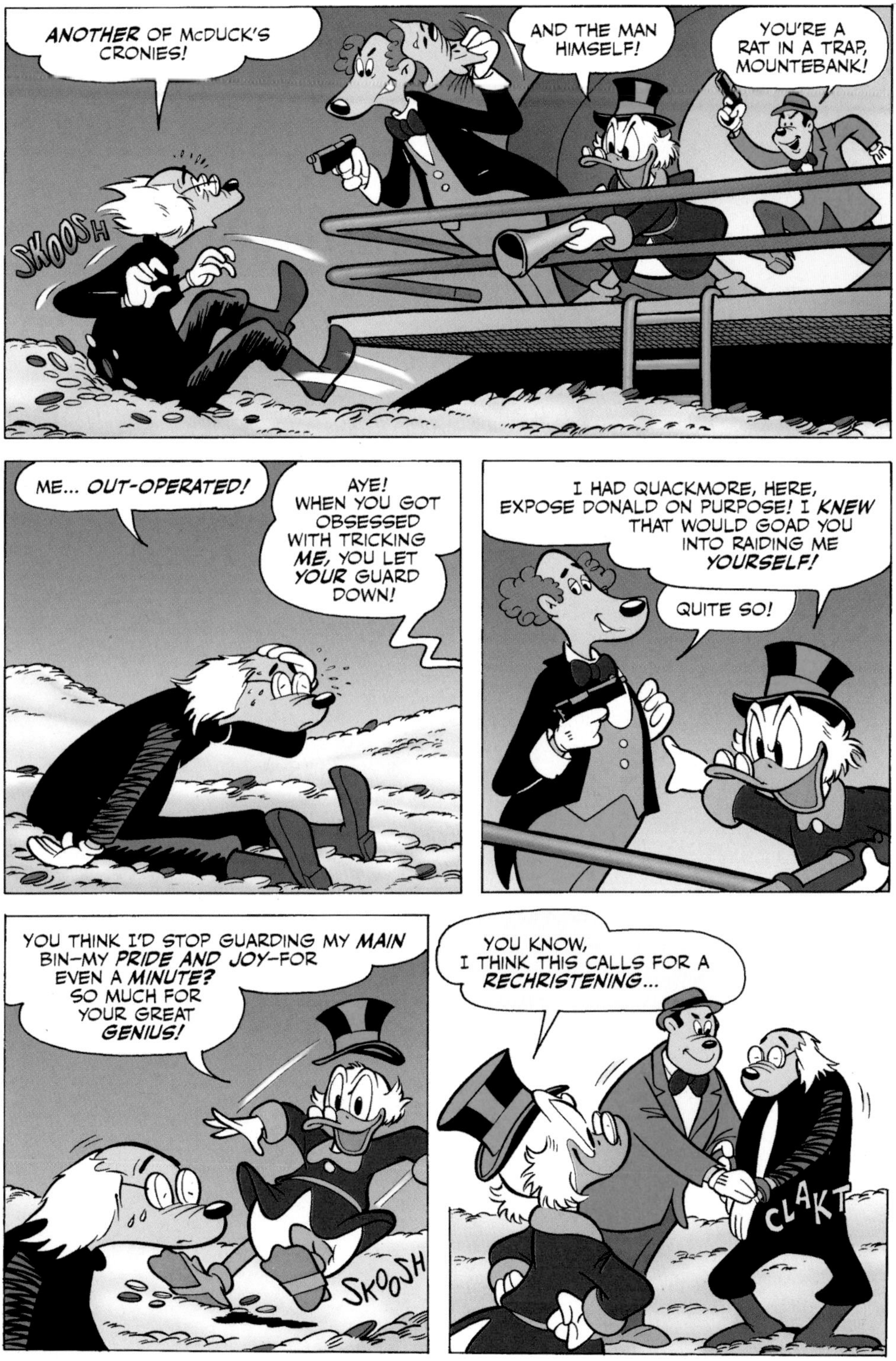
ANOTHER OF McDUCK'S CRONIES!
SKOOSH
AND THE MAN HIMSELF!
YOU'RE A RAT IN A TRAP, MOUNTEBANK!
ME... OUT-OPERATED!
AYE! WHEN YOU GOT OBSESSED WITH TRICKING ME, YOU LET YOUR GUARD DOWN!
I HAD QUACKMORE, HERE, EXPOSE DONALD ON PURPOSE! I KNEW THAT WOULD GOAD YOU INTO RAIDING ME YOURSELF!
QUITE SO!
YOU THINK I'D STOP GUARDING MY MAIN BIN—MY PRIDE AND JOY—FOR EVEN A MINUTE? SO MUCH FOR YOUR GREAT GENIUS!
SKOOSH
YOU KNOW, I THINK THIS CALLS FOR A RECHRISTENING...
CLAKT

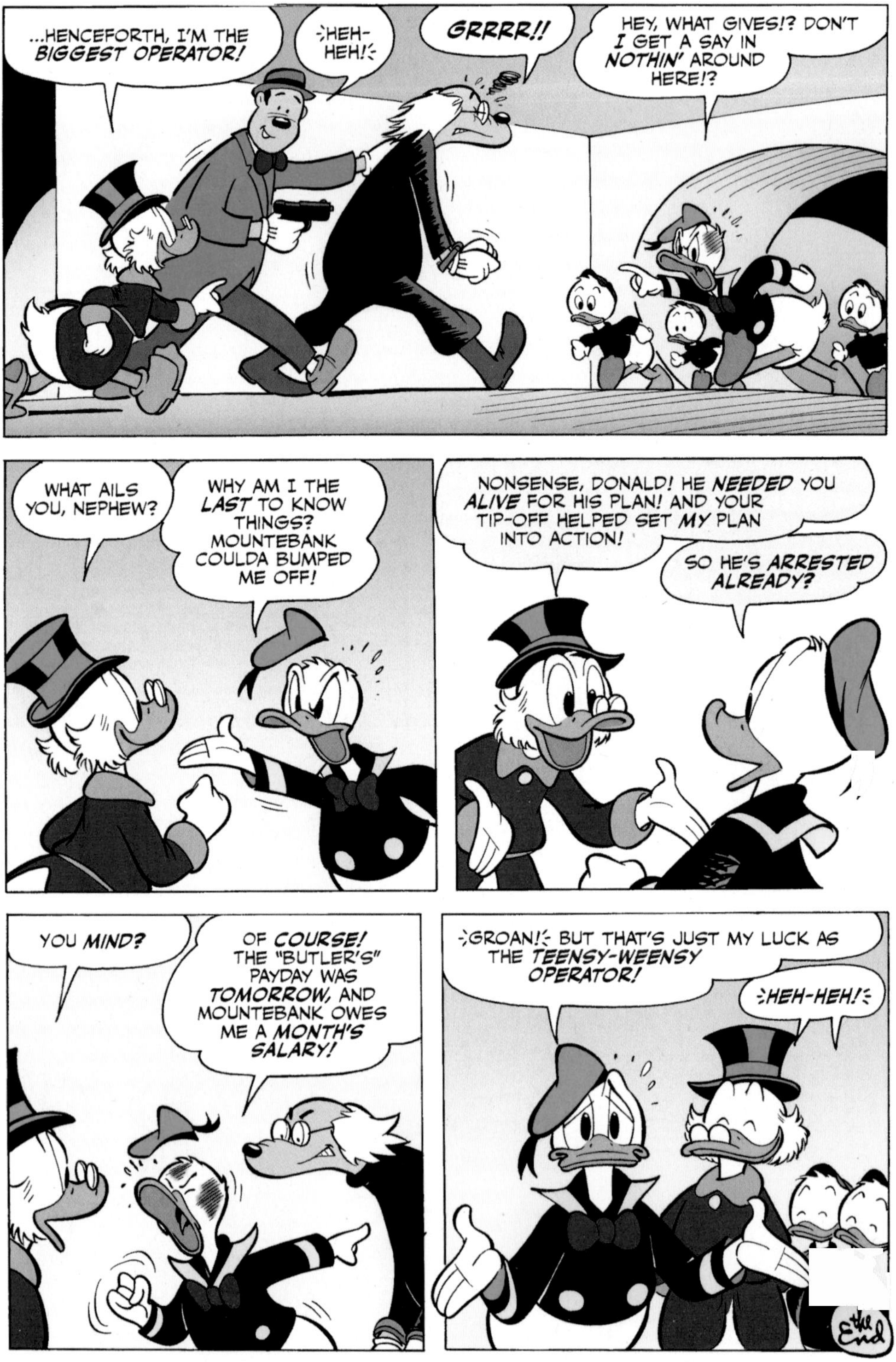

...HENCEFORTH, I'M THE BIGGEST OPERATOR!
HEH-HEH!
GRRRR!!
HEY, WHAT GIVES!? DON'T I GET A SAY IN NOTHIN' AROUND HERE!?
WHAT AILS YOU, NEPHEW?
WHY AM I THE LAST TO KNOW THINGS? MOUNTEBANK COULDA BUMPED ME OFF!
NONSENSE, DONALD! HE NEEDED YOU ALIVE FOR HIS PLAN! AND YOUR TIP-OFF HELPED SET MY PLAN INTO ACTION!
SO HE'S ARRESTED ALREADY?
YOU MIND?
OF COURSE! THE "BUTLER'S" PAYDAY WAS TOMORROW, AND MOUNTEBANK OWES ME A MONTH'S SALARY!
GROAN! BUT THAT'S JUST MY LUCK AS THE TEENSY-WEENSY OPERATOR!
HEH-HEH!
the End

WALT DISNEY'S

UNCLE $CROOGE
in
EXIT the DRAGON

QUIET!

I CAN'T BELIEVE UNCA SCROOGE IS *TREATING* US TO A BEACH TRIP!

MAYBE HE'S *SICK!*

CAN WE GET ICE CREAM, TOO?

NOBODY LIKES A SASS-MOUTH! ICE CREAM... "TREATING" PEOPLE! ⸬FEH!⸬

NO, WE'RE HERE SO I CAN SHOW YOU LADS SOMETHING I RECENTLY HUNTED DOWN!

DO TELL! IS IT CROESUS' *COIN PURSE*, OR MIDAS' MUSTY GOLD *PIGGYBANK?*

YOU *WANT* ME TO HIT YOU.

BUT INSTEAD, I'LL JUST GLOAT!

WAK! A VIKING SHIP!

WOW...

IT'S GOT SOME RELICS ON BOARD THAT I'LL BE EXHIBITING IN MY MUSEUMS. YOU BOYS WILL HAVE THE HONOR OF UNLOADING THEM FOR ME!

FREE LABOR! TYPICAL!

HUH... THIS GOONY GONDOLA IS LOOKIN' MIGHTY *EMPTY!*

SHADES OF GOLDEN HELMETS...

THESE MUST BE THE RELICS UNCA SCROOGE WAS TALKING ABOUT!

NOT THAT *PICTURE!* IT'S TOO *MODERN* TO BE HERE!

HEY, UNCA SCROOGE. THE VIKING IN THIS PAINTING KINDA LOOKS LIKE *YOU!*

⟫ACK!⟪ I DIDN'T MEAN TO LEAVE *THAT* LYING OUT!

GIMME! IT'S PART OF MY... UH... *PRIVATE* COLLECTION!

HUH?

IT'S FROM *CASTLE McDUCK!*

WHAT'S UP, UNCA SCROOGE?

YOU WERE *RESEARCHING* WHETHER THESE RELICS BELONGED TO THAT VIKING, WEREN'T YOU?

WELL, LOOK, I...

WHY?

NERTS! ⟫SIGH!⟪ IT'S MY CLAIM TO THE SHIP. I'LL TELL YOU THE SORDID STORY WHILE WE HEAD HOME. I *TRUST* YOU WELL ENOUGH!

NICE!

ACCORDING TO MY FATHER, THE VIKING IN THAT PORTRAIT WAS AN *ANCESTOR* OF OURS... *DRAGO DRAKESEN!*

"KNOWN LATER AS 'DRAGO THE DRAGON,' HE GREW UP A HUMBLE FARMER IN THE DANISH COUNTRYSIDE..."

SOMEDAY THIS WILL ALL BE *MINE!*

"BUT, ONCE HIS PARENTS PASSED, *DISAPPOINTMENT*... AND DRAGO'S OLDER BROTHER... WERE WAITING!"

SORRY, DRAGO! *I'LL* INHERIT THIS LAND, BECAUSE I'M OLDER AND BETTER-LOOKING!

WHAT!? THAT'S NOT FAIR, BJØRNEFAR! YOU NEVER *WORKED* HERE A DAY IN YOUR LIFE!

"BUT IT *WAS* LEGAL BY DANISH LAW! SO, DRAGO MADE A DECISION THAT WOULD CHANGE HIS AND HIS BROTHER'S LIVES..."

JUST YOU *WAIT!*

"TIT FOR TAT, THE INHERITANCE CHANGED HANDS!"

CONSEQUENCES, SCHMONSEQUENCES! AS LONG AS I'M RICH!

HUH. A QUICK AND EASY PAYOFF!

WAY EASIER THAN SWEATING ALL DAY ON THAT FARM...

"AND SO DRAGO DRAKESEN ACQUIRED A TASTE FOR ROBBING AND PILLAGING!"

BRIGAND! VARLET! THOSE TREASURES ARE MINE!

NOT ANY MORE THEY AIN'T! ⇒HAW!!!⇐

MAAAN, VILLAINY IS TOPS! I'M GETTIN' RICHER ALL THE TIME! BUT IT'S NOT ENOUGH! IT'S NEVER ENOUGH! I CRAVE MORE! MORE!!!

BWAHAHAHA!!!

"DRAGO ROBBED AND PILLAGED LIKE MAD! UNTIL..."

YOU AGAIN?! GET LOST, HERRINGBONE! I HAVEN'T RECOVERED FROM YOUR LAST ATTACK!

REALLY? IT WAS A WHOLE WEEK AGO.

POOH!

WELL, NEPHEW TAILPIN... THIS WELL'S RUN DRY! SO THAT'S THE END O' THAT!

MAYBE IT'S DRY HERE, UNK...

...BUT I BET THOSE LANDS ACROSS THE SEA ARE SOPPIN' WET WITH RICHES APLENTY!

THE SEA! THAT'S IT, BY ODIN!

"AND SO DRAGO THE DRAGON AND HIS AWFUL NEPHEWS LEFT ON THEIR FIRST OVERSEAS PILLAGING EXPEDITION!"

YAAAH! GET LOST IN A TIDAL WAVE, YA CREEPS!

⇒PBBBT!!!⇐

"YEP. DRAGO DRAKESEN *SINGLEHANDEDLY JUMPSTARTED* THE VIKING RAIDS ON EUROPE!"

THAT'S NOT *FAIR!* OTHER VIKINGS PILLAGED US LAST WEEK!

WHAT CAN I SAY, SKIPPY? I'M A *TRENDSETTER!*

I'LL TAKE SARSAPARILLA!

HAW!

HAW!

HAW!

BOYOBOYOBOY! WHAT'LL WE DO WITH THE BOOTY?

WE *STORE IT,* TAILPIN! OTHERWISE WE'LL NEVER GET *RICH!*

SEE? I'VE AMASSED ALL I EVER PILLAGED INTO MY *MONEY HOLD!* MY FIRST GOLD PIECE, MY FIRST CROWN, MY FIRST—

YOU ARE A MENTAL CASE!

THAT AIN'T FOR ME, UNK! I WANNA HAVE *FUN* WITH MY LOOT!

FEASTBURG

EAT! GORGE! REVEL!

HOOEY! PHOOEY! BLOOEY! ...*AWAY!!!*

BUT... BUT...

WELL, THAT'S JUST *SILLY!* SO DID OLD DRAGO GIVE UP ROBBING AND PILLAGING, OR DID HE RETIRE TO FLORIDA IN OPULENCE?

FLORIDA? ZIP YOUR LIP! NO, HE BECAME MUCH RICHER STILL!

"BUT NOW THERE WERE NEW PROBLEMS."

I'M HERE TO ROB AND PILLAGE!

YEAH? WELL, WE GOT *CASTLES* NOW!

SO *NUTS TO YOU,* VIKING!

GADBLAST IT! NOW THEY'RE BUILDING *FORTRESSES!* THICK HIGH WALLS! BRICKS AND MORTAR!

I CAN'T SWORD-STAB *ARCHITECTURE!* WHAT'LL I DO?

"AS DRAGO FELT HIS FINAL DAYS NEAR, HE BOARDED HIS DRAGON SHIP AND SAILED TO THE WEST, AS WAS THE CUSTOM FOR A TRUE VIKING..."

SO LONG!

"WELL, IF YOU CAN'T BEAT 'EM, *JOIN* 'EM! IN 901 A.D., DRAGO SAILED TO THE YOUNG NATION OF SCOTLAND! HE MARRIED INTO A PROUD CLAN—AND TOOK THEIR SURNAME AS HIS OWN..."

THE *CLAN MacDUICH* OF *CASTLE MacDUICH!* AND NOW I CAN STORE *MY* RICHES IN A SAFE PLACE, TOO!

MAKES SENSE! VIKING ANCESTRY IN SCOTLAND RUNS DEEP! BUT WHY SHOULDN'T ANYBODY KNOW DRAGO WAS *OUR* RELATIVE?

'CAUSE HE WAS *JUST LIKE* UNCLE SCROOGE... HOARDING AWAY BULLION IN A TOY FORT, SAFE FROM ROBBERS AKIMBO!

YOU *TAKE THAT BACK!* I'M NO *THIEF-NOTHING* LIKE DRAGO! EVERY CENT I MADE I EARNED *HONESTLY!* IN FACT... PAYING *REPARATIONS* TO DRAGO'S *VICTIMS* WAS WHAT *MADE* THE OLD McDUCKS *POOR!*

OKAY, OKAY!

WE WON'T BLAB TO ANYONE THAT DRAGO THE DRAGON WAS OUR ANCESTOR!

YEAH! WOODCHUCKS' *AND* LITTLE BOONEHEADS' HONOR!

SO NOW CAN WE THREE HAVE ICE CREAM?

WHAT?

ER... MAKE THAT *FOUR* ICE CREAMS. CONSIDER IT A PAYOFF! NATURALLY, *I'LL TAKE* VANILLA...

I GET IT! ≿HMPH!≾

I MIGHT HAVE INHERITED DRAGO'S *HOARDING* SKILL...

...BUT *YOU THREE* INHERITED HIS *PIRATICAL* INSTINCTS!

HUEY! DEWEY! LOUIE! ...*AWAY!!!*

BWAHAHA HAHA!

GET LOST!

UNCLE SCROOGE'S HOME EC 101:

Walt Disney

WINNING WASHOUT

H-2251-04

NOT YET... ANY SECOND NOW...

CARWASH

AT LAST!

:HEH!: BRILLIANT INVENTION, THE AUTOMATIC CAR WASH!

SAFE, QUICK, TIDY—

AND AS LONG AS IT'S HERE, I DON'T HAVE TO PAY FOR DETERGENT!

END

Walt Disney's

GYRO GEARLOOSE

÷HMM!÷ A *CIRCLE* ON THE CALENDAR...

CALENDAR

HEAVENS TO HODGKIN! IS THAT *TOMORROW* ALREADY?!

H 8245

THE ANNUAL *PICNIC* OF THE NATIONAL INVENTORS' SOCIETY! AND THIS YEAR IT'S BEING HELD *HERE*–IN *DUCKBURG!* OH, ME!

AS *TOP* LOCAL INVENTOR, I'VE BEEN NAMED THE OFFICIAL *GUEST HOST!* THAT MEANS *I* MUST UNVEIL A *SPECIAL* INVENTION AT THE BIG EVENT...

THE *MOST GROUNDBREAKING* GADGET I INVENTED DURING THE PAST TWELVE MONTHS! BUT *WHICH* TO CHOOSE?

NOISELESS VACUUM

USEFUL THINGS

EVEN-MORE-USEFUL THINGS

MY AUTOMATED ALL-IN-ONE DUSTPAN AND MOP? NO!

OR MY EXTRA-SENSITIVE *SCALE,* THAT PRINTS OUT THIN PEOPLE'S *WEIGHT* AND FAT PEOPLE'S FAVORITE *RECIPES?*

THINK HARD

BEEF UP!

(LEAVE THOUGHTS HERE)

NOT SO GROUND-BREAKING...

HAVE I LET A *YEAR* GO BY WITHOUT CREATING *ANYTHING* TRULY USEFUL?! ÷GULP!÷

I'M LOSING MY TOUCH! I'LL *NEVER* MEASURE UP TO MY *IDOLS* OF CENTURIES PAST!...

THINK HARDER

BAD IDEAS

LIKE BEN FRANKLIN, DISCOVERER OF ELECTRICITY!

YOWP!

ZAP!

OR GRAHAM BELL, INVENTOR OF THE TELEPHONE!

RING RING RING RING RING RING RING RING

OR THOMAS EDISON, GENIUS OF THE GRAMOPHONE!

SKIP SKIP SKIP SKIP

NO... OF *ALL* MY RECENT INVENTIONS, ONLY THIS *IMPROVED FLYSWATTER* HAS SOLD IN NUMBERS!

WHAT AN AWFUL THING TO BE REMEMBERED FOR! I'LL HAVE TO INVENT SOMETHING *NEW* FOR THAT PICNIC!

KNOCK! KNOCK!

BUT I BET I WON'T—

HI, GYRO! I'VE GOT A *PROBLEM!*

WHAT'S THAT, DAISY?

CUSTOMERS AT MY SHOP SAY OUR *SHOPPING BAGS* ARE TOO *SMALL!* BUT IF THEY WERE *BIGGER,* I COULDN'T STORE THEM UNDER THE COUNTER!

WELL...

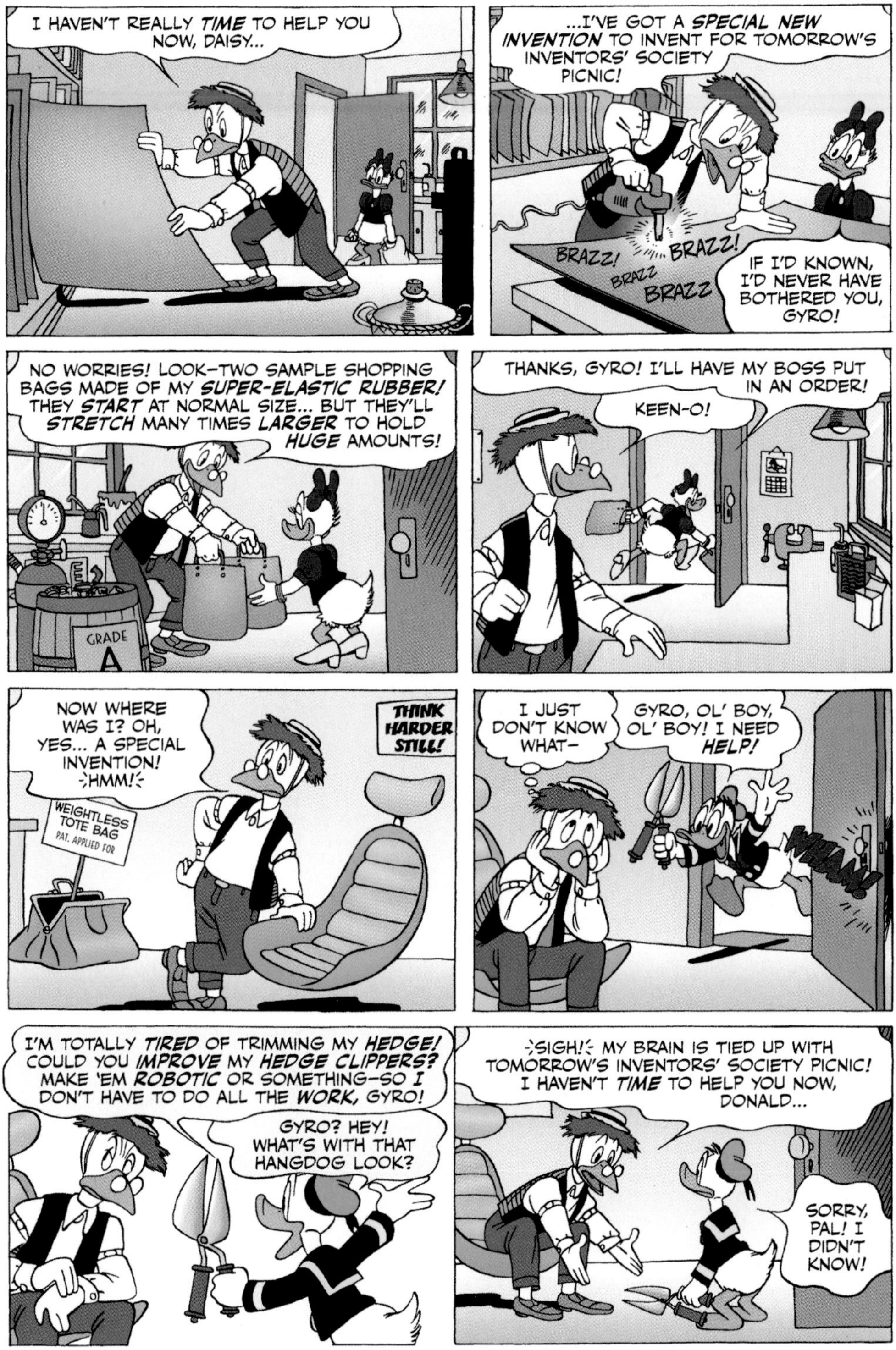
I HAVEN'T REALLY TIME TO HELP YOU NOW, DAISY...
...I'VE GOT A SPECIAL NEW INVENTION TO INVENT FOR TOMORROW'S INVENTORS' SOCIETY PICNIC!
BRAZZ! BRAZZ! BRAZZ BRAZZ
IF I'D KNOWN, I'D NEVER HAVE BOTHERED YOU, GYRO!
NO WORRIES! LOOK—TWO SAMPLE SHOPPING BAGS MADE OF MY SUPER-ELASTIC RUBBER! THEY START AT NORMAL SIZE... BUT THEY'LL STRETCH MANY TIMES LARGER TO HOLD HUGE AMOUNTS!
GRADE A
THANKS, GYRO! I'LL HAVE MY BOSS PUT IN AN ORDER!
KEEN-O!
NOW WHERE WAS I? OH, YES... A SPECIAL INVENTION! HMM!
THINK HARDER STILL!
WEIGHTLESS TOTE BAG PAT. APPLIED FOR
I JUST DON'T KNOW WHAT—
GYRO, OL' BOY, OL' BOY! I NEED HELP!
WHAM!
I'M TOTALLY TIRED OF TRIMMING MY HEDGE! COULD YOU IMPROVE MY HEDGE CLIPPERS? MAKE 'EM ROBOTIC OR SOMETHING—SO I DON'T HAVE TO DO ALL THE WORK, GYRO!
GYRO? HEY! WHAT'S WITH THAT HANGDOG LOOK?
SIGH! MY BRAIN IS TIED UP WITH TOMORROW'S INVENTORS' SOCIETY PICNIC! I HAVEN'T TIME TO HELP YOU NOW, DONALD...
SORRY, PAL! I DIDN'T KNOW!

BUT I'VE GOT SOMETHING *READY-MADE* THAT SHOULD OUTCLASS YOUR HEDGE CLIPPERS!

OBOY!

INVENTIONS WHILE-U-WAIT

HERE YOU GO, DONALD!

EH? LOOKS LIKE A JAR FULL OF *BUGS*!

SOLAR-POWERED *BUGBOTS*... *LIKE* BUGS, BUT WITH BETTER A.I.!

WAK! DO THEY *CHEW UP TREES* LIKE BUGS?

YOU MIGHT SAY THAT! JUST WATCH!

SOON!

SEE? TRIMMED TO PROFESSIONAL PERFECTION! THEN BACK THEY SCURRY, INTO THEIR JAR!

WOWSY! I COULD HAVE A *BOTTLE-SHAPED* TREE! BUT... WHY A *BOTTLE*?

‹HEH!› I *TRAINED* THESE BUGBOTS TO MAKE "BOTTLES" FOR THE GURGLE-URP SODA FACTORY'S LAWN! BUT THEY CAN MAKE *OTHER* SHAPES!

HOW?

?

BY *RETRAINING*, OF COURSE! YOU *TEACH* THEM BY PUTTING THE IMAGE YOU WANT UNDER THEIR JAR-LID... SO!

BOMB-DIGGITY!

AFTER TEN MINUTES OF *STUDY*, THEY'RE READY TO CHEW THE DESIGN YOU CHOOSE!

THANKS A JILLION, YOU *GENIUS*, YOU!

ME, A GENIUS? BAH! A GENIUS WOULD HAVE DONE *THIS* SOONER!

KA-BOP!

CLOSED
DUE TO PICNIC EMERG

THERE! NOW MAYBE I CAN WORK IN PEACE!

A *SPECIAL* INVENTION SHOULD BE SOMETHING THAT *ALL* HUMANITY CAN BENEFIT FROM! AND I'VE GOT EXACTLY *ONE* AFTERNOON AND *ONE* NIGHT LEFT TO INVENT IT IN!

DAYLIGHT SAVINGS OFF

Half a Loaf Is Better Under Deadline

UNIVERSAL CALENDAR

BUT FIRST SOME STRONG COFFEE FOR MY WEARY BRAIN!

COFFEE TEA COCOA SOUP SYNTHESIZER

YECCH! >HM!< MAYBE IF I INVENTED A *BETTER* COFFEEMAKER—

Pride Goeth Before a Patent Refusal

WHAM! WHAM! WHAM!

CAN'T YOU READ SIGNS? COME BACK *TOMORROW!*

I CAN'T *WAIT* THAT LONG! TIME IS *MONEY!* OPEN UP!

OSED T TO NIC GENCY

I'M *BUSY*, MR. McDUCK! IT SAYS SO ON THE DOOR—

"*PICNIC* EMERGENCY!" WHO *CARES?* PICNICS ARE A FOOLISH *WASTE* OF TIME!

CLOSED DUE TO PICNIC EMERG

>SIGH!< FINE! HOW CAN I HELP YOU?

BY MAKING THESE *OPERA GLASSES* STRONGER, LAD!

SO PICNICS ARE FOOLISH, BUT OPERAS ARE A-OK!

BAH! OPERAS ARE FOOLISH TOO—BUT PROFITABLE! SO I PLAN TO INVEST IN A LOCAL OPERA HOUSE...

...AND THAT MEANS TESTING THE QUALITY OF ITS SHOWS! SUPER OPERA GLASSES WILL LET ME WATCH FROM THE CHEAPEST SEATS!

REET!

NOW THESE SUPER LONG-DISTANCE X-RAY OPERA GLASSES WILL LET YOU WATCH FROM OUTSIDE THE THEATRE WALLS! YOU WON'T EVEN HAVE TO BUY TICKETS!

COPACETIC, GYRO! WHAT DO I ¬UGH!¬ OWE YOU?

ALL I WANT IS PEACE... SO I CAN THINK UP A NEW INVENTION FOR TOMORROW'S PICNIC! UNDISTURBED!

IT MUST BE SOMETHING BIG! SOMETHING SPECIAL!

SWELL!

WHEN YOU'VE INVENTED IT, DROP ON BY! MAYBE I CAN MANUFACTURE IT AND EARN A FORTUNE!... ¬KOFF! KOFF!¬ FOR BOTH OF US!

SIGH!

SUNSET! HOURS TILL THE PICNIC... AND DOOMSDAY! BRAINS, DON'T FAIL ME NOW!

ALL NIGHT LONG THE HOMEFIRES BURN AT GYRO'S—AS HE BEATS THE CLOCK TO CREATE THE INVENTION OF A LIFETIME! IS HE EGGHEAD ENOUGH?

MORNING! HUNDREDS OF INVENTORS FLOCK TO THE PICNIC SITE... THIS ISLAND IN DUCKBURG'S VAST TULEBUG RIVER!

FERRY BOATS

GENIUSES IN REPOSE ENJOY IDLE TALK AND A SANDWICH... UNAWARE OF THE GREAT DRAMA ABOUT TO BUST LOOSE!

FINE SPOT FOR A PICNIC, EH, DR. BRAINMORE?

AFFIRMATIVE! ICED TEA COLD ENOUGH?

HEY! IF IT ISN'T, POUR IT INTO MY *SUPERFREEZE THERMOS!* IT CAN CHILL *ANY* LIQUID TO ABSOLUTE ZERO IN SECONDS!

SCIENCE SHIVERS ON!

SO, GEARLOOSE! THE TIME HAS COME FOR YOU—AS *GUEST HOST*—TO SHOW US THE *GREATEST INVENTION* YOU HAVE BUILT IN THE PRECEDING ANNUM!

RIGHT!... ER... I'M AFRAID I DIDN'T HATCH *ANYTHING* GREAT THIS YEAR! EXCEPT THIS BALL OF ⋛GULP!⋛ *UNBREAKABLE STRING* THAT I... WHIPPED UP LAST *NIGHT...* ⋛YAWN!⋛

IS THAT *ALL*?

YOU'RE A *SHAME* TO YOUR CITY, SIR!

NO, HE ISN'T! GYRO IS THE *GREATEST* INVENTOR IN THE *WORLD!* JUST YESTERDAY HE BUILT THESE *SUPER-STRETCH ELASTIC SHOPPING BAGS* FOR ME...

AND THESE *LONG-DISTANCE X-RAY OPERA GLASSES* FOR ME...

AND HE LOANED *ME* HIS *TRAINED BUGBOTS!*

WHO ARE *YOU* PEOPLE? WHAT ARE YOU DOING HERE? ARE *YOU INVENTORS?*

JUST... *FRIENDS...*

WHO HOPED TO MAKE A *DIFFERENCE!*

IT'S NOT ENOUGH! ⋛SIGH!⋛ THE GADGETS I GAVE YOU WERE BASED ON *OLD IDEAS—TOO OLD* TO QUALIFY FOR TODAY'S DEMO! AND NOT *GOOD* ENOUGH, ANYWAY!

THAT'S RIGHT!

IT'S MY DUTY, AS GUEST HOST, TO UNVEIL AN *EXTRA-SPECIAL* INVENTION TODAY! AND MY BRAIN JUST HASN'T REACHED AN EXTRA-SPECIAL LEVEL LATELY! WOWSERS!

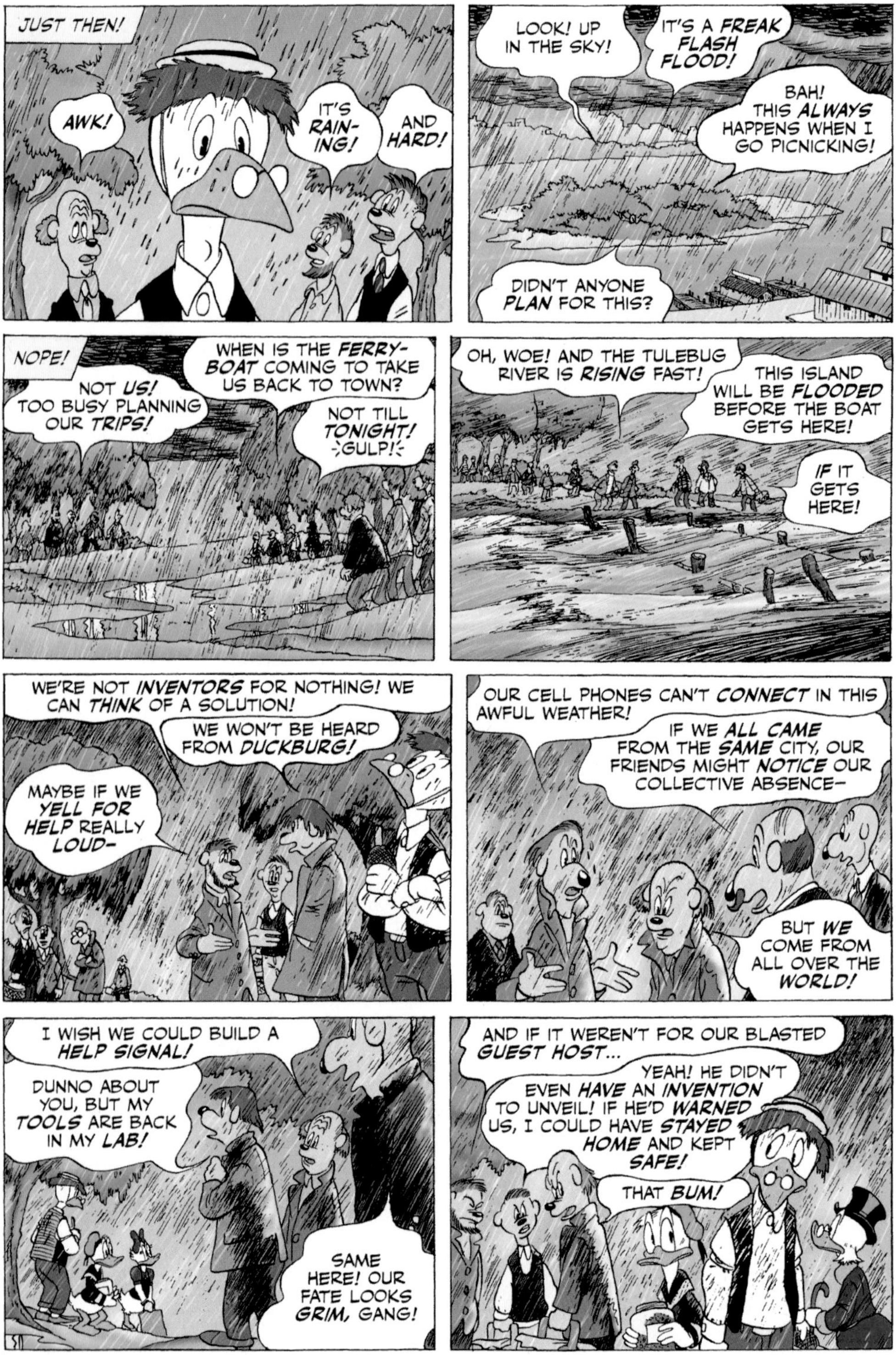
JUST THEN!
AWK!
IT'S RAINING!
AND HARD!
LOOK! UP IN THE SKY!
IT'S A FREAK FLASH FLOOD!
BAH! THIS ALWAYS HAPPENS WHEN I GO PICNICKING!
DIDN'T ANYONE PLAN FOR THIS?
NOPE!
NOT US! TOO BUSY PLANNING OUR TRIPS!
WHEN IS THE FERRYBOAT COMING TO TAKE US BACK TO TOWN?
NOT TILL TONIGHT! GULP!
OH, WOE! AND THE TULEBUG RIVER IS RISING FAST!
THIS ISLAND WILL BE FLOODED BEFORE THE BOAT GETS HERE!
IF IT GETS HERE!
WE'RE NOT INVENTORS FOR NOTHING! WE CAN THINK OF A SOLUTION!
WE WON'T BE HEARD FROM DUCKBURG!
MAYBE IF WE YELL FOR HELP REALLY LOUD—
OUR CELL PHONES CAN'T CONNECT IN THIS AWFUL WEATHER!
IF WE ALL CAME FROM THE SAME CITY, OUR FRIENDS MIGHT NOTICE OUR COLLECTIVE ABSENCE—
BUT WE COME FROM ALL OVER THE WORLD!
I WISH WE COULD BUILD A HELP SIGNAL!
DUNNO ABOUT YOU, BUT MY TOOLS ARE BACK IN MY LAB!
SAME HERE! OUR FATE LOOKS GRIM, GANG!
AND IF IT WEREN'T FOR OUR BLASTED GUEST HOST...
YEAH! HE DIDN'T EVEN HAVE AN INVENTION TO UNVEIL! IF HE'D WARNED US, I COULD HAVE STAYED HOME AND KEPT SAFE!
THAT BUM!

EGAD! I CAN SEE MY *MATTRESS FACTORY WAREHOUSE* THROUGH THESE SPECS! STORMY *WINDS* BLEW THE *ROOF* OFF THE WAREHOUSE! WHAT A DISASTER!

DISASTER?!

GLORYOSKY! I'VE *GOT* IT! DONALD, GIVE ME THE LID OF THAT BUG JAR!

WHAT HAVE YOU GOT, GYRO?

A *PLAN* TO GET US *RESCUED!*

WITH *WHAT* TOOLS? YOUR *STRING* CAN'T *TOW* US TO SHORE!

BUT A FEW MINUTES LATER!

WHAT ARE YOUR *BUGS* DOING TO THAT *TREE,* GEARLOOSE?

CHEWING IT INTO A SHAPE I CHOSE... WHILE *I* SLICE DAISY'S SUPER-ELASTIC BAGS INTO *STRIPS!*

SOON! HE'S TIED THE STRIPS INTO A *GIANT* STRIP... AND IS *FASTENING* IT TO THE TREE'S TWO REMAINING BRANCHES!

WHAT *IS* HE UP TO?

NO STORMY IDEA!

HERE, DAISY! I'VE TIED MY UNBREAKABLE STRING TO MY BELT! WILL YOU HOLD THE *SPOOL* SECURELY FOR ME?

CERTAINLY, GYRO!

SOME KIND OF *CATAPULT...?*

NOW! IF *YOU* SIRS WOULD BE SO GOOD AS TO PULL ON THIS *ROPE...*

IT'LL NEVER WORK!

THE WIND WILL BLOW HIM RIGHT *BACK!*

I'M USING THE OPERA GLASSES TO TELL THE *PRECISE* LOCATION OF MR. McDUCK'S WAREHOUSE! AIM A BIT MORE TO THE *RIGHT...* JUST A BIT...

-NNGH!- WHAT A *STRETCH!*

HUFF! PUFF!

I CAN'T KEEP THIS UP MUCH LONGER!

FIRE!

WOING!

AND NOW, IF MY CALCULATIONS WERE *CORRECT*...

WHOOSH!

YES!

PLOOF!

MCDUCK MATTRESS CO.

HUZZAH! A FOUR-POINT LANDING! AND NOW GYRO IS FASTENING A *STEEL CABLE* TO THE UNBREAKABLE STRING!

REEL HER IN, DAISY!

ROGER!

THE CABLE IS SOON HITCHED FAST TO A *STURDY OAK ON THE ISLAND!* THEN GYRO SENDS A JURY-RIGGED SKI CHAIR BACK AND FORTH TO RESCUE HIS IMPERILED PEERS!

RIGHT *NICE* OF THAT BOY!

MR. GEARLOOSE, OUR *WORTHY* COLLEAGUE... YOU *SAVED* OUR LIVES! INESTIMABLE *THANKS!* YOU'RE A *REAL* GENIUS!

I'VE NEVER *SEEN* SUCH *QUICK* INVENTIVE INSTINCT!

WE'RE *SORRY* WE TREATED YOU SO *RUDELY*, GYRO!

GYRO RESCUED HIS *REP* ALONG WITH HIS COLLEAGUES' GOOD HEALTH!

HOW DO YOU THINK HE FEELS?

›HEH!‹ LIKE A *NEW MAN!* EVEN IF MY DAY-SAVING INVENTION WAS ALSO BASED ON A VERY *OLD* IDEA...

WHATCHA THINK, CHUB? CAN I HIT HIS SILLY *HAT* IN *ONE SHOT?*

THE END!

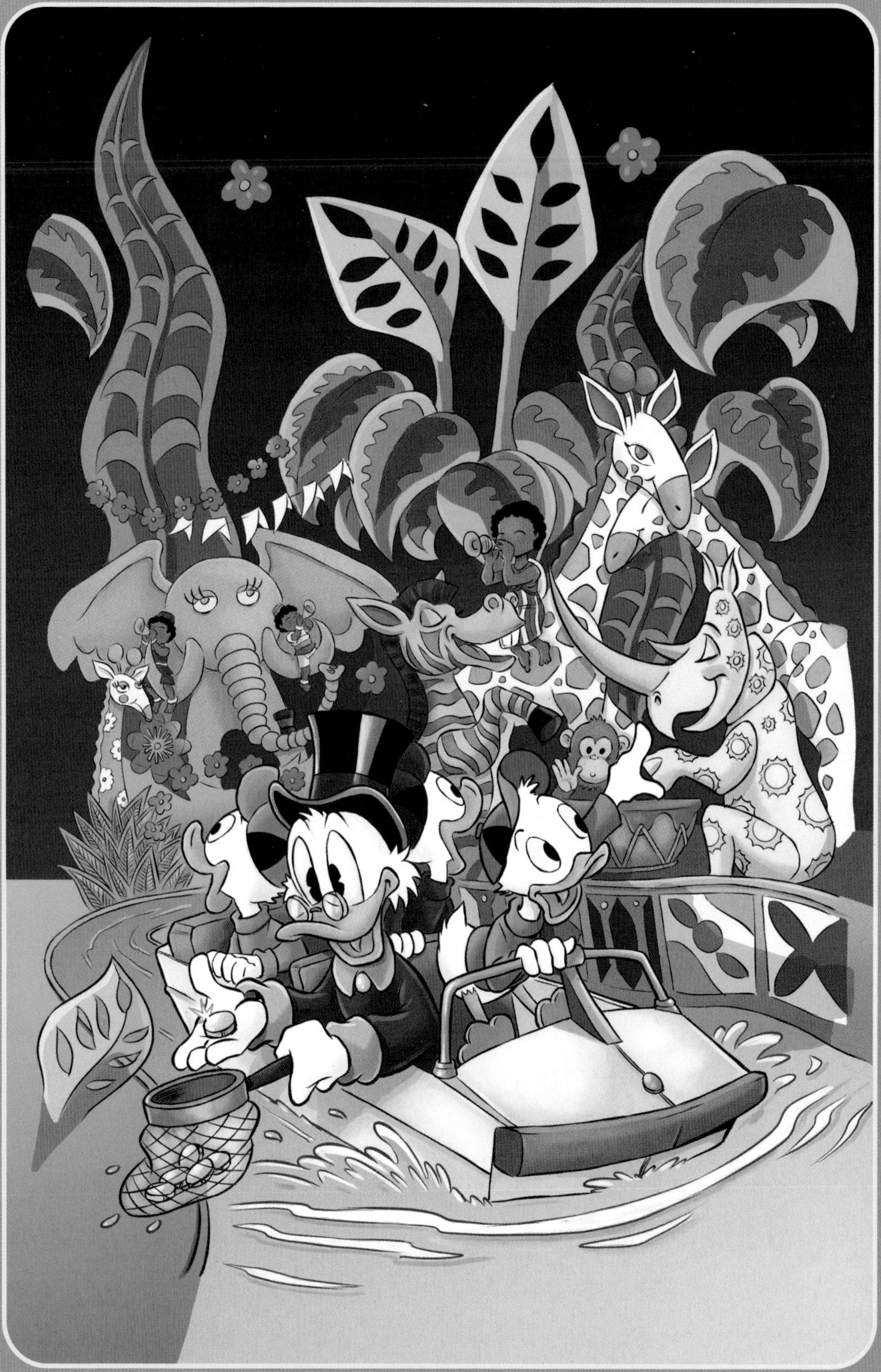

Art by Thom Pratt

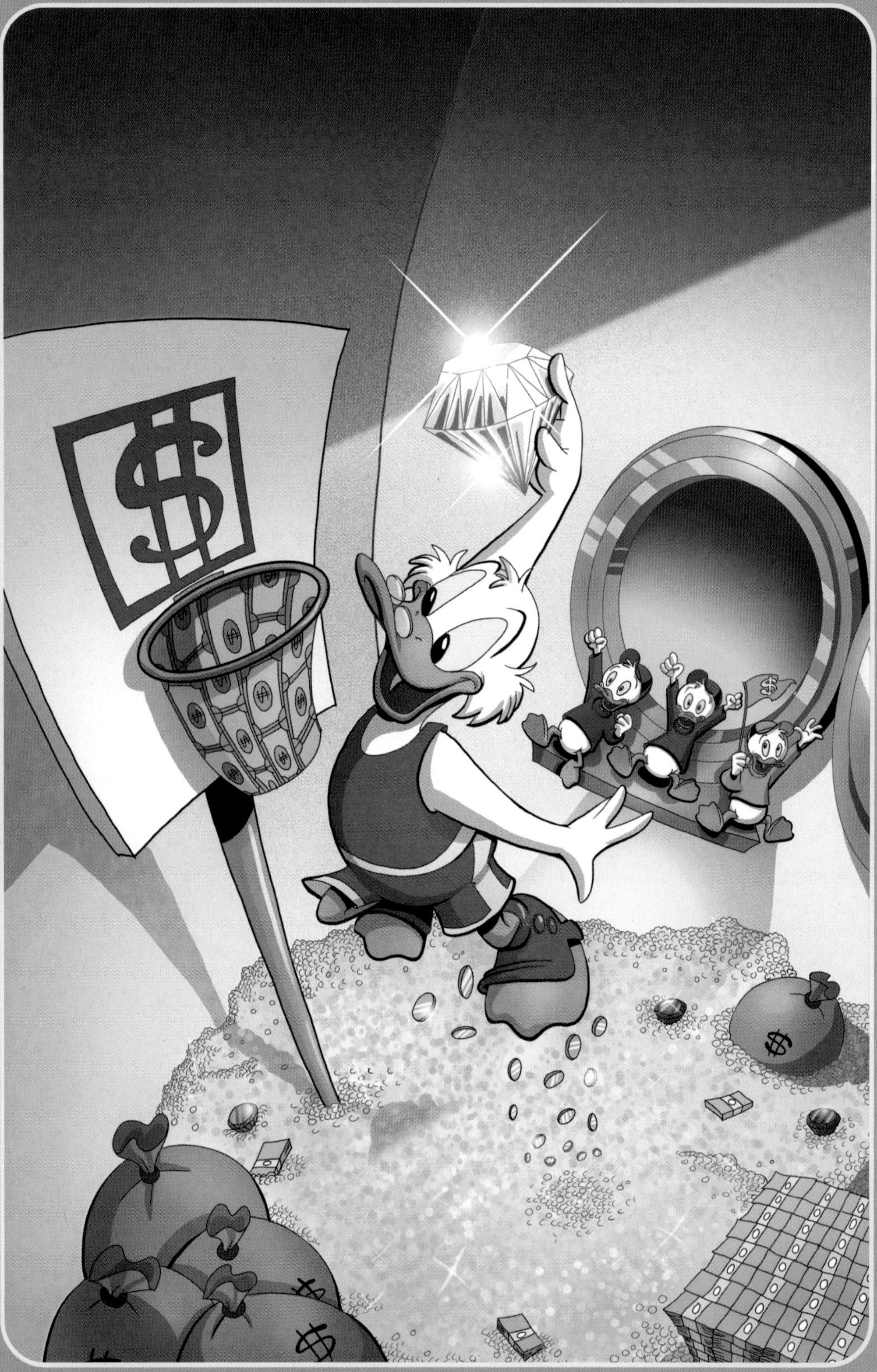

Art by James Silvani

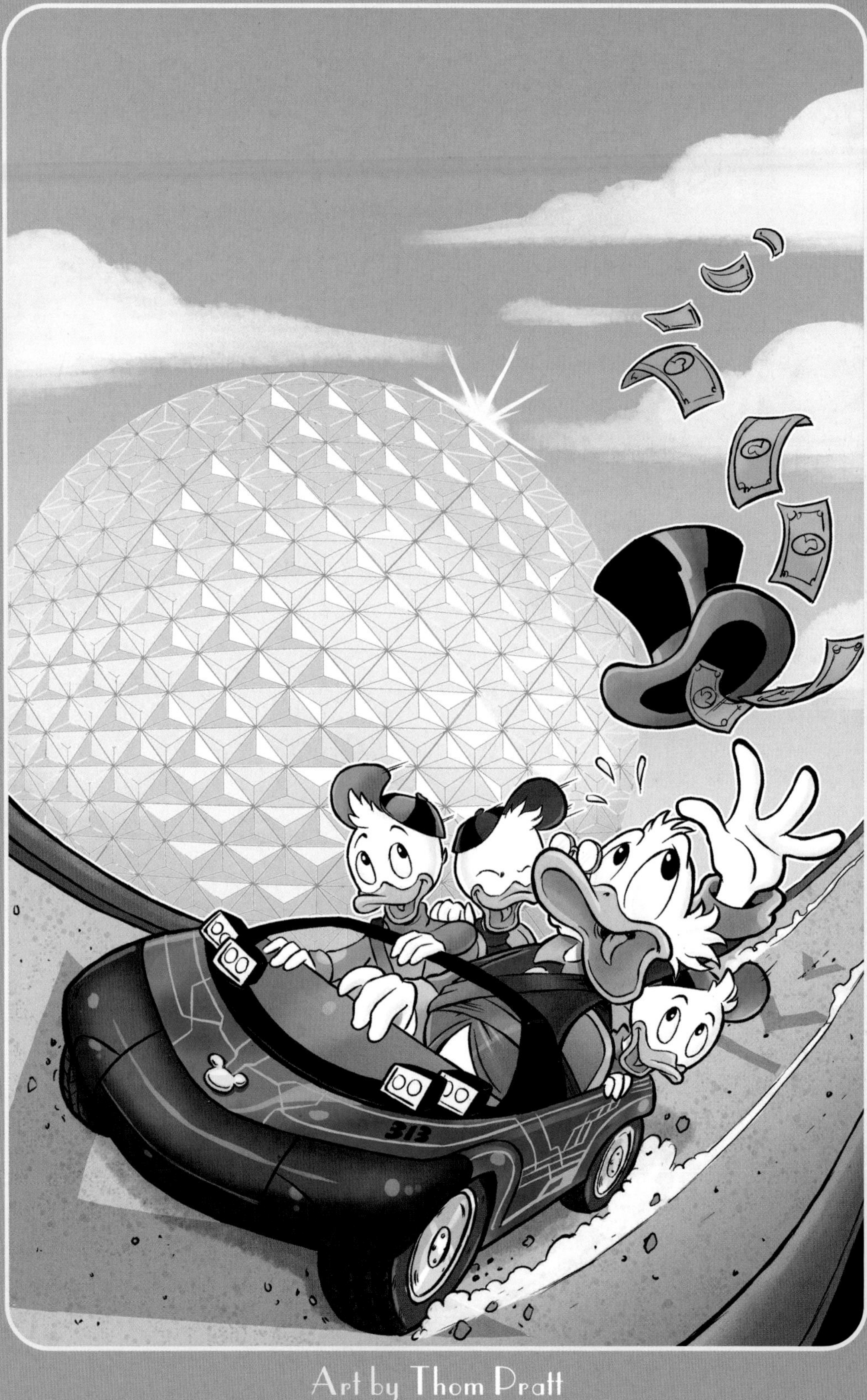
313

Art by Thom Pratt

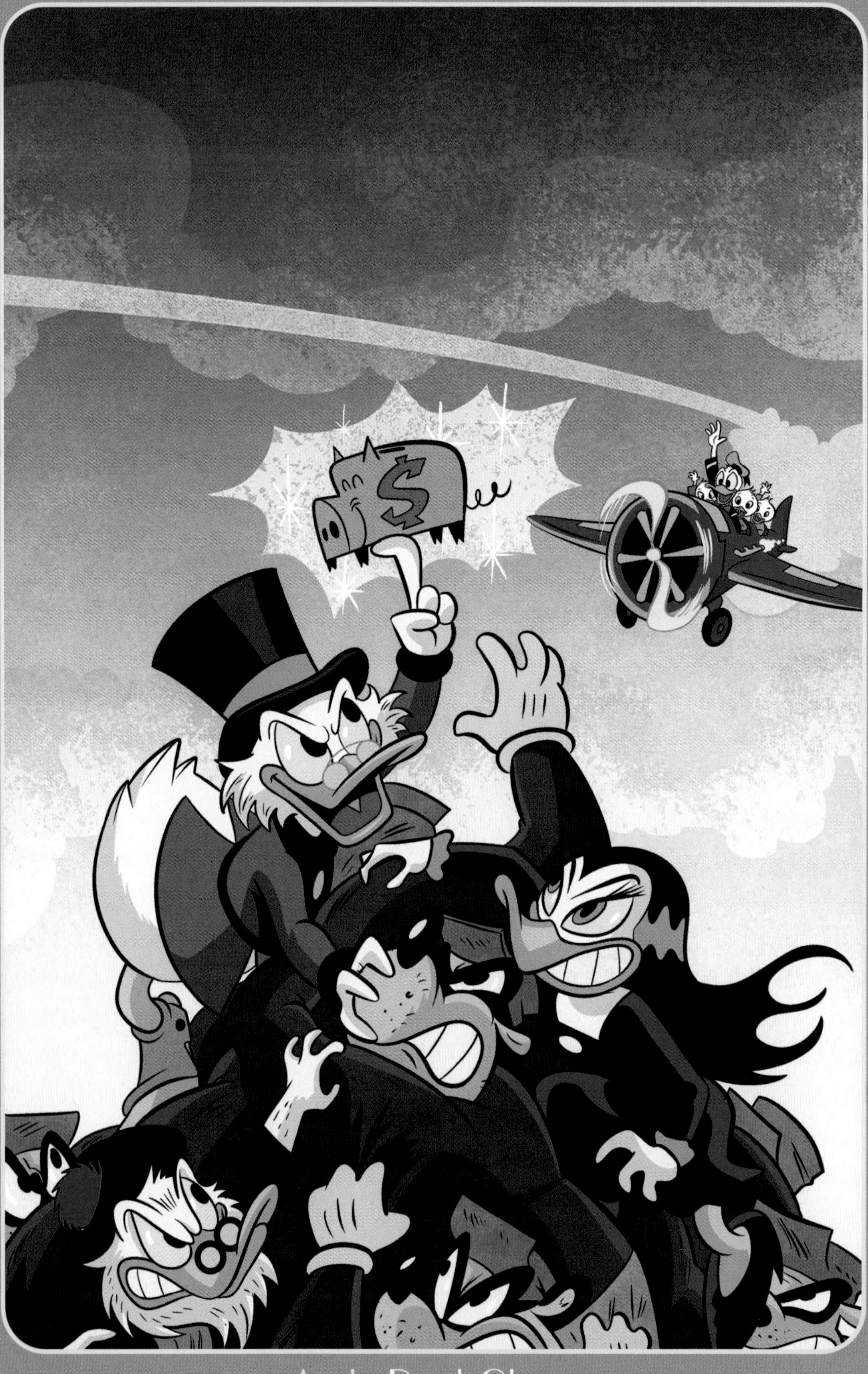

Art by Derek Charm

Art by Jonathan H. Gray, Colors by Ronda Pattison

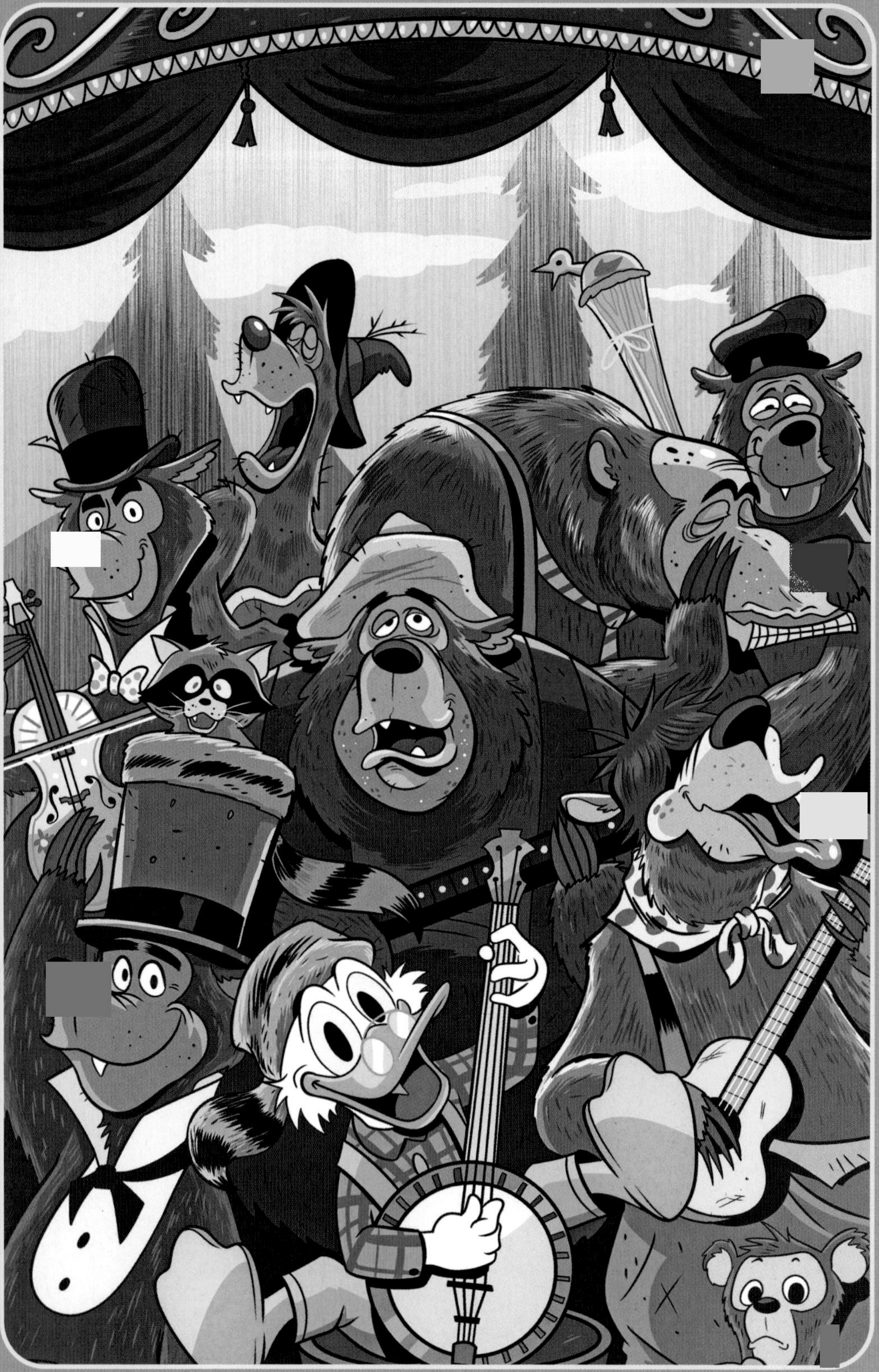

Art by Derek Charm

Art by Amy Mebberson, Colors by Derek Charm